THE STOLEN THRONE

THE VILLAINOUS REIGN SERIES

IVY COLE

Map of the Kingdoms

Playlist

Survivor by 2WEI, Edda Hayes
I'm Yours by Isabel LaRosa
Arcade by Duncan Laurence
Lovely (with Khalid) by Billie Eilish, Khalid
Luminary by Joel Sunny
Power Over Me by Dermot Kennedy
Castle by Halsey
In the Name of Love by Martin Garrix, Bebe Rexha
Iris by The Goo Goo Doll
Silence - Illenium Remix by Marshmello, Khalid, Illenium
Monsters by Katie Sky
Train Wreck by James Arthur
Infinity by Jaymes Young
Stay Alive by Hidden Citizens, Black Clouds
Lion by Saint Mesa
Morally Grey by April Jai
Royalty by Egzod

DEDICATION

To those who fight their own battles every day. We are often the villains in our own stories.

But just think, a hero without a villain is pointless; a villain without a hero is successful.
So, be the villain of your own story. Success awaits you.
The heroes in your story are the haters who wish to see you fall.
PROVE. THEM. WRONG.

Special Shout-outs

To Aron - Thank you so much for helping me with this story! You really helped me bring the king alive. I hope to have you help me with other books in the future!

To Dani - A reader turned true friend! I'm so glad I met you! I hope you continue to enjoy my books wifey!

To Cheryl - Thank you for author-napping me! You have been an amazing PA, and I can't possibly thank you enough!

To my Alpha's - I couldn't make these books as amazing as they are without you. Thank you!!!

Content Warnings

This book contains many dark themes. There will be mentions and scenes with the following:

Death

Blood

Torture

Knife play

Mentions of rape. Rape

Sexual assault

DubCon

Bodily fluids

Sex

Bondage

Death/Killing

War/Fighting

Graphic death

Murder

Physical assault

Scars

Stabbing

Torture

Morally Gray characters

IVY COLE

CONTENTS

PROLOGUE

*W*e are all the villain in someone's story, the hero in others. It all depends on who is telling the story. This... this is my story. I'll let you decide if I'm the hero or the villain.

"Daddy!"

The dark-haired man turns, his smile hidden under his beard as he laughs. "My Little Snowflake."

He catches me as I jump into his arms, giggling. My mother chuckles beside him as she tries to reprimand me. "Eira, you must act like a proper princess."

My father holds me close and says, "Nonsense. She has only a few more years before she comes of age. Let her act like a child a little while longer." He presses a kiss to the top of my head. "You are growing so fast, daughter. I must enjoy it while I can."

"I suppose you have a point, husband. Thirteen will come quickly, and childhood will soon be forgotten." My mother pinches my cheeks before pecking my father on his. "I will handle today's duties. Enjoy your time with our daughter before you must leave."

My eyes widen at that news. "You have to leave?"

He sighs and replies, "I must visit Cybele. We need to solidify our treaty with the country."

"Why can't someone else go?" I whine.

He chuckles. "I am the king, my Little Snowflake. The kingdom will be yours one day. I have to ensure it is at its best for you."

"I'll be queen!" I squeal happily.

He boops me on the nose. "Yes, you will." He lowers me to the ground before kneeling himself. Now at eye level, he continues, "It is necessary that you remember to protect the people. They will be your responsibility one day."

My head tilts in question. "How do I do that?"

He smiles. "You are a snowflake in this world. Pure and delicate. One of a kind. But you must also remember that even if you are delicate, that does not make you weak. Kindness and love are not weaknesses."

I nod, my curls bouncing as I do. "I need to be kind."

"I have no doubt you will be." He sighs before wrapping me in his arms. "You won't understand this now, but one day you will. As a ruler, you will have to make hard decisions. Do things that are distasteful. You will need to do what's best for everyone, not just one person. You must always do what is right."

My small hands pat his back. "It's okay, Daddy. You and Mommy will be here to help me."

His hold on me tightens. "Of course we will."

"I'm not scared, Daddy."

He pulls away with a smile. "My fearless snowflake."

Little did I know that would be the last time I saw my father. The last day I would hear him calling me his Little Snowflake.

CHAPTER ONE

Seated in my father's chair, I swing my legs back and forth. His desk is large compared to my thirteen-year-old self. But my mother needs help to run the Kingdom of Arcelia. My father disappeared years ago, so he's no longer around to help. I am the *only* heir, much to the disappointment of my mother's advisors. They believe a king should sit on the throne instead of a queen.

That means my luxurious life as a Lady of the Court will never be. My lessons became focused on the nuances needed to rule. Finance, the art of arbitration, the state of the kingdom and its surrounding nations; these are now a permanent part of my life. The advisors wanted me kept in the dark, to turn me into their puppet with a crown who dances on their strings, but Mother wouldn't allow it. If I am to be Queen of Arcelia, it is important for me to learn these things.

However, tensions with the neighboring Kingdom of Wylan lead me to believe that there may not be anything left for me to rule over. I have never met the King of Wylan, but I have heard many stories. A despicable man filled with nothing but greed and death. He lays waste to any who oppose him.

We have only been able to keep them at bay because the number of soldiers we have far surpasses theirs. I am not sure how long that will last, though.

He sounds like one of the villains I used to read about in my stories when I was younger. But this is not a fairy tale. My father's words about doing what is right are ingrained in my brain. But I wonder if there is a difference between doing what is right and doing what is necessary. Is doing what is necessary always right? Is doing what is right always necessary?

My mother often said that I was still a child, and it would take time for me to understand adult concepts. Is it wrong of me to question things? Why don't adults question things more often? Would a villainous dictator be ruling over Wylan if the adults had questioned things more?

Huffing out a sigh, I focus back on a map of the four kingdoms. We have solidified alliances with Islwyn, but their neighboring Kingdom of Cybele is another story. Arcelia has no issues with Cybele at the moment, but they are currently being bombarded by those trying to flee Wylan. Which will put a strain on their resources.

It will also give Wylan the perfect opportunity to invade. Which means we need to help fortify Cybele's borders to prevent Wylan from taking control of their kingdom. *Hum... What should we do?*

I jump when I hear a knock on the door. Looking up from the map, I see my lady-in-waiting smiling in the doorway. "You have lessons, Princess."

I nod and push away from the desk. Jumping up from the chair, I smooth out my dress to ensure I'm wrinkle free. It won't do for the future queen to arrive at her lessons wearing a wrinkled dress. I need to think like the prince my parents never had, while also looking like the presentable princess they *do* have. Somehow, I need to fill both roles.

Giving myself one last look, I say, "Let us be off, Charlotte."

She follows behind me as we make our way down the hallway. "Do you have any notes for me to take to the queen, Princess?"

I sigh. "I have ideas, but the advisors won't go for them. I'm starting to think that because I do not have a dangly thing between my legs, my words fall on deaf ears."

"Princess," Charlotte hisses.

"What?" I huff. "Is it not true?" She opens her mouth to repeat the same words she always does. I interrupt her before she can say any more. "Do not say it is because I am young. My age would not matter if I were male."

Her eyes soften as she says, "They will regret not listening to you one day."

"Let us hope it is before my people are killed. Apparently, when the King of Wylan kills, it matters not if they have a penis or a vagina."

Taking one last look at Charlotte, I give her a nod before entering the room where several teachers are waiting. My mother believes I deserve the best education. Which meant a different teacher for each subject.

Taking a seat at my desk, I ask, "What will I be learning today?"

One of the silver-haired women steps up, giving me a bow. "We will be learning a few dances today."

Arching a brow, I ask, "Dancing?"

Her eyes meet mine as she replies, "Yes, Princess. The queen's advisors believe it is important due to your age."

My eyes narrow. "The advisors requested I learn to dance?"

Her eyes lower to the floor as she nods. "Yes, Princess."

I look around the room at the other teachers before asking, "And if I wish to learn something else today?"

"It would be inadvisable to do so, Princess," she answers quietly.

"What would a prince be learning, I wonder?"

A gentleman in the corner replies, "It is unimportant to know what a prince would be learning, Princess."

I rise from the desk, standing as tall as my thirteen-year-old frame allows. "Do not dismiss me because I do not have a penis, sir. I am just as capable as a prince."

His eyes immediately fall to the floor as he nods. "Yes, Princess. I did not mean to imply…"

"There seems to be a lot of that going around," I interrupt. "Now, I will be continuing with the lesson plans from the original schedule. I will no longer be underestimated."

"Yes, Princess," the room replies in unison.

I am tired of the kingdom's advisors trying to push me out of the role I was always meant to hold. I am the Princess of Arcelia, and it is about time people started treating me like the future queen I will be. That was what my father wanted for me, and I won't stop until I fill that role.

Chapter Two

"Are you serious, Mother?!" I scream as I throw my notebooks across the room. Loose papers fly out as the notebooks thump onto the floor.

Four years. Four years of studying and learning as much as possible about the kingdoms and their people; all of it for nothing. The advisors have given up, and so has my mother. My mother, the Queen of Arcelia, has decided to bend to the wishes of the King of Wylan.

"Eira! Settle yourself," my mother commands.

"Settle myself?" I yell back at her. "Settle myself! You decided to hand our kingdom over to the biggest tyrant known to man, and you want me to settle?!"

Her eyes narrow on me as she says with conviction, "I am doing what is necessary!"

I scoff. "You are doing what is easy, not what is right. You have chosen not to fight for our kingdom and her people to protect them from that man."

She turns away, huffing out a sigh. "You are too young to understand the matters of adults."

"It is not hard to understand that you are handing over our kingdom to the man who invaded Cybele because we did not aid them! He has Islwyn in a choke hold, and still, you do nothing." I throw another notebook across the room. The thump of it hitting the wall echoes around the room. "Suddenly, you agree with the advisors and have come to blame my age. You refuse to take my advice seriously. Father would have taken me seriously."

Her eyes blaze, and her tone changes. As if dealing with a petulant child, she replies, "Your father is not here!"

I point a finger at her as I scream, "Exactly!"

Her eyes widen. "Eira?"

My eyes burn as my anger begins to overflow. "Father is not here but you are. You are here! You are supposed to protect this kingdom, but you have done nothing. You have allowed the advisors to cloud your thoughts! You allow them to rule the kingdom instead of you. Father would be ashamed of you for giving up on our kingdom and its people."

She sighs heavily in exhaustion. "I am trying, Little Snowflake."

I suck in a breath as the tears begin to fall. "Do not call me that."

She winces at the venom in my voice. "I am trying to rule this kingdom the best I can. I can only do so much."

I turn away, shaking my head. "You caved to the power of Wylan just like everyone else."

She sighs before I hear her retreating footsteps. Her heels click across the hardwood floor with each step. "I hope one day you will understand. The wedding will be held tomorrow evening. He will be here only for the wedding before returning to Wylan. He has allowed us to keep the castle."

I let out a bitter laugh. "How gracious of him." I listen for the click of the door closing before I look back. She doesn't understand, and how could she? The loss of Dad was as hard on her as it was on me, but that doesn't mean she should allow those men to tell her what to do.

They hate that she is in charge instead of a man, and they use every opportunity to throw it in her face. My anger wasn't directed toward her; it was toward them. The men who constantly remind her that she could never lead this kingdom as well as a man could. They finally convinced her to cave and marry the very man we have been fighting against to save our kingdom.

I snort out a laugh as I look around the room, now covered in notebooks, journals, and loose papers. My mother shouldn't bow to those men. She's the damn queen. They should be listening to my mother and me, not the other way around.

Huffing out a sigh, I kneel down to pick up each notebook with care. All this work and research for nothing. Years of drawing up plans to fight the King of Wylan, all wasted.

There's a knock at the door before it opens. I look up to find Charlotte, her eyes wide when she sees me on the floor picking up my things. "Princess." She rushes over to help me with the rest. "I see it did not go well."

I let out a humorless laugh. "I feel as if most of my conversations with my mother do not go well, Charlotte."

She hums as she says, "She shoulders many burdens."

Gripping the notebooks tightly, I murmur, "She would not have to shoulder so many alone if she would allow me to help."

Charlotte gives me a sad smile. "She wishes to protect you. She loves you very much." Her voice quiets when she says, "Those men are quite distasteful."

I laugh. "She should have removed them the moment Father died. They have done nothing to help. Only stating again and again that she cannot rule as well as a king could."

She holds out a stack of my papers. "Do you think the King of Wylan will keep his promise?"

I arch a brow in question. "To allow us to keep our castle?"

She nods. "And allow us to live?"

Huffing out a sigh, I shrug. "I'm not sure. From what I have learned over the years, he does not keep many people around who could challenge his power."

Her eyes widen. "Do you think he will kill us?"

I set the notebooks aside and grip her hands in mine. My voice is determined as I reply, "I will protect you all as best I can."

She gives me a soft smile. "I believe that is something we should be saying to you, Princess."

I shake my head. "It is my duty as princess to protect all my subjects. No matter their station."

Her grip on my hands tightens. "Then we shall protect each other." She gives my hands another squeeze before releasing them. "Well, I suppose we should get this mess cleaned up."

I take another look around the room and groan. "I did not realize how many I had thrown. So many loose papers to pick up as well."

She chuckles as she stands and holds a hand out for me. "It will be quite the distraction until morning comes. You will have to sort what papers go to which notebook."

I roll my eyes but smile as I take her hand. "Then it will be a welcome distraction. That man is the last person I wish to think about this eve."

Pulling me to my feet, she mirrors my smile. "Then I shall supervise. That way it will take longer."

I laugh, shaking my head, as I move around the room, picking them all up. "You can pick out my dress for the wedding, if you wish."

She claps her hands in delight, then rushes off to my closet. "I will make sure you do not upstage the queen."

Chuckling, I continue the long task of gathering my things. Even if my mother marries that man, it does not mean I have to stop fighting.

I will do everything I can to ensure my kingdom does not fall like all the rest.

CHAPTER THREE

What a strange wedding day... I am seated in the front row, unable to comprehend the sight of my mother standing alongside my greatest fear. The nave of the church is dressed in reflections, ornate mirrors and polished silver decorating the space...

The nauseous feeling in the pit of my stomach does not fade as my mother stares into the eyes of the king who has killed so many. No, it seems to grow worse with each word she utters.

"I promise my heart to you, King Balor—"

Does she not see the darkness surrounding the king? The smell of rot and decay seeping from his pores. He smells like death, but it seems that I am the only one who feels uneasy. No one else appears to see the gleam in his eyes as my mother hands him the keys to the kingdom before their vows draw to an end.

That gleam frightens me even more when he turns his gaze from my mother to look straight at me. This is the first time I've seen Balor, the King of Wylan, an utter brute of a man who looks like a bear squeezed into fine silk, in person. But his eyes look wrong, they hold no color except a metallic gray. They look like mirrors...

I tear my eyes away, stopping on one of the many mirrors that line the walls as decoration. Balor must have forced my mother to have them put up because she usually has better taste. I look at myself in the mirror and shiver because, for just a second, I see my reflection mouthing something I cannot hear yet somehow understand. She is telling me to run.

The moment the officiant pronounces them husband and wife, the world explodes. Fearful gasps pull my gaze from the many mirrors, only for me to wish I had listened when she told me to run. I stand frozen as I watch the new King of Arcelia plunge a dagger into my mother's throat.

Chaos erupts around me, but my eyes are locked on my mother as she lets out a soundless scream. Their lips are still touching as blood pours from my mother's throat. I see the dagger, curved and wicked, ripping through my mother's soft skin.

Her white gown quickly turns crimson as he nearly cuts off her head. The way he flourishes the dagger sends a spray of blood into the priest's face just before the point is driven into his eye. The priest and my mother fall into a heap on the ground.

The world seems to slow down around me as I stand frozen; the only thing I can hear is a ringing in my ears. Hands land on my shoulders and forcefully turn me away from the horrific scene. Charlotte stands in front of me, wide eyed and screaming, but it takes what feels like forever to hear what she is saying.

"Run, Princess!"

I'm shocked out of my daze by the deafening screams around me. I look around, my eyes widening as I watch the mirrors all over the room shatter, turning into swirling portals of shimmering glass. Wylan soldiers begin pouring through, cutting down any who try to resist. But that isn't what catches me so off guard. It's the fact that every single soldier looks identical: dull gray skin, emotionless faces, and eyes like balls of glass.

Through my shock, I feel Charlotte dragging me toward the doors. Roaring laughter jerks my gaze back to the new king, and I see mother's blood dripping down his face, his blade held high above him.

"Arcelia falls tonight!" His gaze finds me in the chaos, and his smile turns sinister before he shouts, "Worship me!"

The room erupts with replies of, "All hail our God, King Balor!"

I take in the room around me and realize the only people who reply are the king's undead soldiers. Blood covers the wooden floors as my eyes meet the king's once more. He steps down from the altar and yells, "You cannot run from a God." Someone screams beside me, followed by the sound of more glass breaking. Looking over, I find Charlotte in Balor's grasp, his blade having pierced her chest.

"Charlotte!" I scream as her hand slips from mine. Balor's tongue, still covered in my mother's blood, licks Charlotte's ear before he lets her fall.

I can't breathe, my lungs refusing to inhale. The new King of Arcelia smiles down at me with his hypnotic, mirrored eyes. "You are my prize. The precious Snowflake of Arcelia. Mine to put in a globe and shake as I please." He runs his thumb over my lips leaving some of my mother's blood behind. "I'll enjoy making you dance atop my miniature tower."

Fear, pain, and loss twist inside my broken heart, quickly morphing into anger. "At least you admit that it's miniature—" I hiss as I slap him across the face. He doesn't even move to avoid the impact, but then my arms are wrenched behind my back. "A little frost bite isn't going to hurt me, Princess."

Something feels wrong with my legs. I begin to panic when what feels like giant worms slither up my legs, gripping my calves under my dress. I'm forced to my knees, and the way they slowly creep up my bare legs makes me feel somewhere between being tickled and being violated.

I want to laugh, cry, something! My knees crunch against broken glass, cutting through my dress and slicing my skin. I know I'm bleeding, so I look down to check, only to take in what's happening.

Where Balor's shadows obscure the light; the shattered mirror shards reflect his dark countenance and exude black tendrils that begin to form larger tentacles. Black smoke shifts into liquefied-glass state, reflecting me obscenely upon their surfaces before moving to restrain my arms and slide beneath my dress.

When I look up, cold, reflective eyes are peering down at me. His smile widens as he slides the smooth side of his blade across my jaw and down the center of my chest. He smears my mother's blood across my skin only to stop at the neckline of my dress. I see him tremble with excitement, and it makes my stomach twist. "I do hope you bleed as beautifully as your mother did. I wonder if your screams will be as delightful."

I let out a screech as he drags the knife down the center of my dress, parting it to reveal my undergarments, and I stare down in horror at the tentacles of mirrored glass that wrap around my waist. I want to cover myself, but my hands are restrained, so I'm forced to watch the tentacles push up under my bra. I try not to make a sound, not wanting to give him any satisfaction, but I can't help my squeal of surprise when my bra is ripped apart.

I close my eyes, feeling the tentacles wrap around my breasts. They squeeze, and I feel something I've never felt before: a pressure growing just below my stomach. It doesn't feel bad, and that terrifies me.

Balor steps closer to me, the smell of iron overwhelming. He runs the tip of the knife down my chest to my abdomen, stopping just above that strange sensation.

"Are you going to kill me?" I whisper.

"Why would I kill a prize like you? No." He drags the knife back up to my breast before saying, "I'm going to have my fun with you." He presses the tip of the blade into my nipple just hard enough to be uncomfortable but without drawing blood.

"Scream for me."

He digs the knife in further, and I bite my lip so hard I taste blood as I attempt to keep the scream inside. He laughs and removes the knife. "Still have some fight left in you, I see. Good, you will be fun to break."

When the pain subsides, I glare up at him. "Never!"

He licks my blood from his knife and grins. "Never say never, Little Snowflake. You will break, just like your mother did, all you need is time."

"I'll die before I let you break me," I sneer.

He shrugs and walks away, calling over his shoulder, "You will break either mentally or physically. It matters not which it is." He gives me a wicked wink. "I do hope you last long enough for me to give you to my son, though."

With a gesture, Balor commands his tentacles to move. I squirm as they lift me off the ground, a single tendril sliding under what remains of my undergarments with a soft snap. Then I am left naked several feet in the air.

I look down and see a wriggling pile of tentacles on the ground, a hundred reflections of my body made into something monstrous. It moves forward, randomly grabbing at the ground to pull it, and me, toward the doors of the chapel. The tentacles clutching my body tighten with every little movement, the ones on my breasts sliding over my nipples.

Don't feel it, I think, *don't make a sound.* I try to focus on anything besides the tingles of sensation traveling down my body. *How can he say such cruel things? Treat me like an object, a toy to give his son after he does... what? What is he going to do to me? Why do my legs feel cold... and wet?*

Balor stares at the giant double doors, continuing his villainous monologue without even turning to look at me. "Yes, my son will appreciate you as much as I will, especially after I've trained you to be a good bride for him." He twists his hand in a gesture, and the tips of the tentacles holding my hips move further between my legs.

I cry out as they vibrate against a part of me I never thought about. The sensation makes my brain burn, an explosion that makes everything fade away for just a moment. When the world comes back into focus, my stomach twists at the sound of Balor's laughter.

"That won't be too hard to accomplish."

Tears run down my cheeks, and I keep my gaze pointed on the floor. I barely register the horror that crawls out of the pile of tentacles below me as skeleton arms rip their way free from the mass, a skull made of glass silently screaming as it fights its way out. The shape is hard to see through my puffy eyes from sobbing, but when something sharp like needles scratches my feet, I turn my focus on it.

I recognize the crystalline copy of a bear pelt covering the skeleton's back. The fur is made from thin glass needles, and I cannot lift my legs to keep them from poking my toes. I remember seeing a man like this once, a huntsman who was hired to travel with my father.

Giant bone fingers seem to reach for Balor, only to move past him and grip the doors. They are ripped apart in a frenzy that causes the skeletal huntsman to shatter. The new king walks to the chapel, me following behind against my will.

When I manage to peer through the wide-open doors leading out of the chapel, I let out a gasp. The once luscious lands of rolling green grass and colorful flowers are now a monochromatic wasteland. My kingdom... My family... Gone... All in a matter of minutes.

"I do hope you love the change of scenery," he taunts with a laugh. After walking down the steps, Balor stops. Something else begins to take shape from within the mass of tentacles, something not as horrifying. The shape of a woman rises, and I can't help but gasp at her beauty.

Her face, crafted in mirrored skin, looks at me with sadness. Her body is stretched, seeming to melt endlessly back into the wriggling pile beneath me. She moves *around* me, removing the tentacles that hold me.

Yet I do not fall, my restrained arms shifting from behind me. The strange mirror-woman holds my hands, manipulating my arms to stretch out, as her body curves into a seated position. There I sit, on display, staring down at what remains of my people.

Glass soldiers made from the broken mirrors corral them and force them to look up at me. "Why?" I whisper. Balor hears me, though, walking back up the steps with his dagger pointed toward me. He taps the underside of my chin with the tip of the blade.

"You will find that in this world there are no such things as heroes and villains. There are people who let their morality dictate if they do something or not. They often let things go, blaming their morals. Then there are those who do what needs to be done no matter their morals."

"Which one are you?" I ask, genuinely wanting to know why he is such a monster. Balor's smile fades away, and he stares into my eyes for a long time before he replies.

"A hero would have married your mother, promised you peace and strength. A hero would have loved you like a daughter, raised you to be just as good. A hero would not have hired a huntsman to assassinate your father."

Balor tosses the dagger away. For just a moment, I think I see... something in his eyes. But then the mirrored finish fades, and I look into human eyes filled with... nothing. Completely void of emotion. He grips my throat, whispering in my ear as spittle sprays onto my cheek.

"A villain would fuck you right here, force these people watch as I make you scream. A villain would slit your throat, drink your blood, and laugh. A villain would sit on the throne and make you their queen on a leash."

With a wave of his hand, the glass soldiers massacre my people below. The blood of men, women, and children sprays everywhere, desecrating the church steps. I scream and beg for him to stop, but he doesn't. They stab, slash, and stomp until nothing remains but bloody piles of meat smeared across the ground.

When they eventually stop, and the ringing in my ear fades, Balor speaks, his voice empty of all emotion.

"I am neither."

Darkness falls upon the Kingdom of Arcelia, leaving behind nothing but a barren wasteland because of a heartless king's whims. Rot gives way to much harsher forms of life, weeds and thorny vines creeping across the once lush landscape. Empty cities turn to overgrown ruins, save for the castle that was once my home... Now nothing more than a tomb of my broken innocence.

CHAPTER FOUR

Ugh. How long has it been since I've seen the outside world? Not that I really want to see the outside, but this near-constant dark cell has me second guessing myself. Do I really want a reminder of what my kingdom looks like now? Hum... no. I think I'll pass. My days consist of staring at myself in the mirror above my cot. I hate mirrors. Dark memories try to seep in, and I thump my head against the bed to push them away. I don't want to remember.

I hear a clunk down the hall, and I know it must be time for the day guards to take over. How do I know it's daytime, you may ask? Well, I happen to see a brief sliver of light that shines down the hallway during shift change. It's also the only way I've been able to keep track of time. Otherwise, it's dark and dreary all day... every day.

I hear a guard groan as he stands. Always predictable. "Have a great day, Henry!" I say in a false, cheery voice. I don't know if that's his name, but it's the name I've given him. He looks like a Henry, or maybe a Paul... hum. Maybe I'll change it up tomorrow.

The guards mutter greetings to each other as the door shuts. "Morning, Charles." He doesn't respond... like always. Again, that's not his name, but they've never once introduced themselves in the four years I've been stuck here. Though, I didn't really expect them to, considering they are only here to make sure I'm kept alive. Hum...

I suppose that answers my question. I haven't seen the outside world in four years.

I rub at my wrists, the metal chafing my skin. I hope the king doesn't come by today. Though I doubt he will skip it. Since sticking me here, he's never once skipped a day of trying to break me. To be honest, I'm getting tired. So tired I wish he would just kill me already.

I stiffen when I hear a clang against the door. It's as if my thoughts summoned the man I wished to avoid. I hear his mumbled words to the guard before the door shuts. They always leave. The guards never stay when he's around, which I think is a copout. As if not being here gives them some sort of pass because they aren't here to physically see or hear what is being done to me. Self-righteous pricks.

There's a tap on the metal bars of my cell, but I refuse to look in his direction. I may want to give up, but I'll never give him that satisfaction.

"Little Snowflake, Little Snowflake," he singsongs. "Have you melted yet?"

I hold up my middle finger, and he roars in laughter. "I'm so glad I get to play with you again. You have lasted so long, but I wonder if today is the day."

"Never."

I hear the whine of the metal door to my cage opening, and he enters before closing the door behind him. He even locks it to make sure I can't escape. Again. I've only managed it once, but that was all he needed to ensure he locks the door behind him each time.

My body stiffens as I sink into the bed as much as possible as if to disappear. But it never stops him, and I never disappear. I flinch as his shoes scrape across the floor with each step. "Should we summon them today?"

My eyes flick up to the ceiling to see the mirrored surface begin to waiver. My image morphs in the reflection as it begins to melt into tendrils. I whimper when the tendrils fall to the bed beside me, and I squeeze my eyes shut when I hear him move closer.

I refuse to open my eyes, even when I feel the cool touch of the mirror's smooth surface. The tentacles seem to vibrate with power as they brush across my skin. Think of better days Eira. Your body may be stuck here, but that doesn't mean your mind has to be.

He tuts, and I feel the cold tip of his knife slide across my chest, further reminding me that I'm completely naked. "Open your eyes, Little Snowflake."

I HATE it when he calls me by the name my father used as an endearment. It makes the beauty of the nickname feel dirty and poisoned. It no longer holds the sweet and loving memories of my father.

My eyes shoot open when I feel the knife pressed deeper into the skin of my thigh, and the tendrils slide across my breasts. They massage my mounds, and I bite my lip, refusing to make a sound. I hate that these things bring my body pleasure as he watches. I hate my body's reaction, no matter how much I try to force it to do otherwise. My eyes meet his dark, mirrored pits as he smiles down at me. "There you are, Little Snowflake. Are you ready to have fun today?"

I gather all the spit I possibly can, which is proving difficult, considering how dry my mouth is. Taking a deep breath in, I shoot the glob of spit into his face.

Black smoke begins to swirl around him, and his smile darkens. "So glad you haven't lost your fight. It wouldn't be fun otherwise." He quickly reaches over to tighten the shackles attached to my ankles and wrists.

I hiss as my limbs are stretched out as far as possible, giving him access to every inch of my body. He taps the tip of the knife to his lips while his eyes roam over my body. When his eyes meet mine again, they seem to ripple with power. "I do hope I can make you scream."

Before I can reply, I feel his knife slice my thigh. I bite my lip to keep the screams inside as he continues to make small cuts down my thighs. A tentacle slides between my legs as the others caress and massage my body. The tip slides between my folds, pressing softly on the sensitive, peaked flesh. I feel a gush between my legs when the tentacle presses hard on my sensitive nub. My lips are split and bleeding from me biting them so hard. But no matter how hard I try to keep the tears in, they fall anyways. I hate that my body betrays me like this. That I somehow find pleasure from this torture.

I feel him looming over me as his tongue laps the side of my face. "I do love the taste of your tears, Little Snowflake. Like the sweetest of tarts. Your pain is so delicious." He pulls back, and I allow my eyes to open just enough to see him licking my blood off the knife. His eyes roll back, and he groans. "Your blood tastes exquisite. I can't imagine anything tasting as heavenly as you. My own personal dessert. I am going to miss our sessions together."

My eyes widen at his words, and he laughs. "I did promise to give you to my son. I am a man of my word, after all. I do hope he enjoys you as much as I have."

Panic bubbles up in my chest. No. No. No, no, no, no! I'd rather stay with the villain I know than be handed off to a male I know nothing about. His son could be worse for all I know. He must see the panic in my eyes because his smile grows wider. "He does make me proud. He rules Wylan for me while I am here. I'm sure you will enjoy your new home."

He snaps his fingers, and one of his favorite guards comes around the corner. "I know you love your sessions with me, but I figure it's only fair to let your favorite guard have one last taste as well."

Shit. Shit! Go to your happy place! I hear the click of the door, signaling it's unlocked before it clicks closed again. I feel his disgusting eyes roam over my bloodied and bruised skin. I flinch when I feel his fingers slide over my thighs.

I hear the shifting of clothes, and I can't stop the images of having to watch his pants drop to the floor before each session. I hold myself back from saying how I wish the tentacles would stay between my legs instead of this horrid man. At least with the tentacles I can pretend they don't matter, that it doesn't mean anything. I bite my lip again, feeling the guard's thumb circling my entrance before pressing inside me. I squeeze my eyes shut tighter when I hear another set of clothes hit the floor.

The tentacles slither up my body to caress and play with my breasts as the guard grunts. He continues to slide his thumb in and out of me. "She is just as tight as yesterday, My King. Always so tight."

"Fuck her already before my son gets here. I wish to come before I must greet him," the king says and grunts.

I feel the guard's cock press against my entrance, and I know he will be just as rough as he was yesterday. Like he is every day. I also know that the tentacles are going to pleasure me until I come, whether I want to or not. It's as if the tentacles know I need to be wet enough to handle the guard's rough fucking.

He slams into me with a satisfied grunt and begins to fuck me fast and hard. I hear his panting and grunting as his grip on my thighs tightens.

The tentacles cup my breasts while another slides between my legs to play with my sensitive nub. I feel my body betraying me; I never want to come for this man, for these disgusting tentacles. I can't stop my body from begging for satisfaction, though. Begging to find that release, which allows me to slip away from this horrid place for a few blissful moments. It makes me want to vomit each time.

He growls as he continues to thrust into me, then suddenly pulls out and comes all over the lower half of my body. A tentacle slides in to replace him, humming inside of me as its slick surface strokes in and out. I grit my teeth as it hits just the right spot, and I come. I hold back a whimper as it slides out of me, circling my sensitive nub once before all the tentacles retract.

The guard groans. "It's a pity you agreed to give her to your son. She's the best fuck I've ever had."

The king shouts, and I feel his hot release coat my chest. He pants as he replies, "If the others do not satisfy me the way she does, I will steal her back." He chuckles as they get dressed. "You look so good covered in our release, Snowflake. Best clean you up before my son sees, though."

He and the guard chuckle before I hear the clank signaling that the door is opening and closing. I watch the tentacles slither up the wall and slip back into the mirror above me. I wait until I hear the outside door close behind them before I let a sob slip out, biting my lip to suppress any others from escaping. I stare at my reflection in the mirror, tears streaming down my face, covered in blood and cum. I can't even wash it off because the king didn't release my wrists.

Please... someone... anyone. Please save me from this hell.

CHAPTER FIVE

The feel of clothes against my skin is odd, considering I haven't worn any in so long. Feeling clean is another oddity, but the king didn't want me covered in crusted cum and dirt when he presented me to his son. I shuffle my way down the hallway of the prison that has been my home for the last few years. I never thought I would be free of this place. This wasn't what I had in mind when I thought of escaping, though. Gifted to the king's son like I'm an object to be possessed.

I squint as I leave the dark hallway and step out into bright sunlight. It takes my eyes a moment to adjust, having been kept in the dark for so long. The guards tug me along as I try to make out my surroundings. Everywhere I look it's a blackened wasteland. So it wasn't a dream. My chest tightens at the thought. What once was the lush greenery of Arcelia is now withered and gone. Staring down at the ground, lost in my thoughts, I'm suddenly jerked to a halt.

Still looking down, I see the hooves of a horse enter my immediate view. I slowly peer up to find a man staring down at me with arched brows. He surveys me as if accessing my value. I bristle under his gaze but refuse to say anything with the king watching.

"You didn't tell me I would receive a raven, Father."

The king chuckles and replies, "She's more like a snowflake. She's delicate and melts so prettily for me."

A male behind the prince laughs and speaks up. "She seems more like a fearful Snow Bunny, Your Highness."

I see the quirk of his lips before the prince scowls. "Yes. Well, all I see is a raven. Though I think she's forgotten how to fly."

The king chuckles darkly again. "I've made sure to clip her wings. I can't imagine her flying anytime soon."

The prince tilts his head as he continues to stare at me. "Shame. I think the chase would be fun." He looks over his shoulder, then calls out, "Branimir, ensure the carriage is ready. We leave immediately for Wylan."

The king bristles and frowns at his son. "You brought a carriage for her?"

The prince shrugs. "I have to make sure my little raven isn't taken from me. Would be a shame to lose her after you so graciously gifted her to me."

The king seems to settle at that. "You have a point, son. Well, I must be off. Things to do."

The prince gives him a sharp nod and waits until his father is out of sight, then his whole demeanor shifts. He looks around, making sure none of his father's men are nearby, then turns to the man who called me a snow bunny. "Asher, get her into the carriage as soon as possible," he says in a hushed tone.

His gaze briefly shifts to me before he turns to one of his other men. "Reverie, check to see if we have any extra food rations for her. My father obviously treated her like one of his pets."

The male nods and rides off. I watch as the man he called Branimir comes up riding a horse that is pulling a small carriage. I watch as another male jumps down from his horse and makes his way over to the carriage.

He opens the small door and turns to me, gesturing me inside with a wink. "Your carriage awaits."

I hum but remain where I am. "Who are you?"

He looks to the prince, awaiting his approval. The prince looks at me before giving the man a nod. Turning back to me, the man gives me a smile and says, "My name is Alair, Princess."

I arch a brow as I slowly move over to the carriage entrance. Reverie jogs up, holding out a small bag. "There isn't much, but that's all the food we can spare right now. You'll have access to more once we get back to the castle."

After a moment of hesitation, I reach out for the bag and jump when I hear someone speak up behind me. "If the prince wanted you dead, he would have shot you with an arrow. He wouldn't make you suffer through poisoned food."

I look over my shoulder to find a man with dark, shoulder-length hair and a well-groomed beard. I dare to take him in for a second. He's wearing normal guard attire, but I can see hints of black swirling around the collar of his shirt. Is his body marked? Curiosity flares within me as I begin to wonder how much of his body is marked. I haven't met many males who have 'inked', I believe the term is, their bodies. I shift my gaze to meet his, and his dark hazel eyes seem to pierce straight through me. I'm frozen under his stare and jump when I hear the amusement in the prince's voice. "Kasim, stop scaring the girl."

I bristle as I retort, "I am not a girl; I am a woman." With a huff, I grab the bag from Reverie. I'm about to step into the carriage when my guilt over snatching the bag out of his hand takes hold. Years of manners, even if I haven't used them much lately, have a death grip on me, making me turn back around.

My cheeks heat when his eyes meet mine. "Thank you for the food."

He gives me a jerky nod and turns to hop back onto his horse. Biting my lip, I turn back to find Alair offering a hand to help me into the carriage. He gives me a smirk and asks, "Should I fear you slapping my hand away?"

I roll my eyes but slip my hand into his; I am grateful for the help. I try to put on a brave face, but my energy is severely depleted from the years of being held captive by the king. "As long as you do not touch me without permission you will be fine."

He gives me a nod. "Noted."

Once I'm inside the carriage, he closes the door behind me. Open windows allow me to see outside and feel the fresh air but, to be honest, I'm more interested in the food I've been provided.

I pause when I hear one of the males I haven't been introduced to yet say, "We will need to close the windows the moment we cross the border, Prince Dax."

The prince huffs out a sigh and replies, "I understand, Benidict. I know what could happen if she's exposed."

The male lets out a sigh of his own. "I do hate when you use our full names."

Dax laughs. "Well, I hate using them. But we aren't safely at home where rank does not matter."

The carriage begins to move, and I'm met with silence. I'm not sure I'm supposed to hear Benedict's reply when he says, "I do not believe this is a good idea. It's not safe, and she does not seem educated on how the world works now."

I bristle at his words. What does he mean by that? I'm plenty educated about our world. I made sure to learn everything I possibly could about the surrounding kingdoms.

The man named Dax hums as he rides just in front of the carriage. "Do you think I should have left her with my father?"

"No, but..." he trails off before continuing, "she will view you the same way she views your father."

"And how is that, Bene?"

"A bastard, or worse, a villain."

Dax is quiet for a moment before he replies, "I will always be the villain in someone's story. You know I have never minded that role."

I think it odd that Benedict seems upset by the thought of Dax being a villain. He *is* the villain; do they not see the darkness swirling around him? Do they not see what his father has done to the land? I do not know what power the king possesses that causes the land to decay the way it does. But I know his son has that same power. Eventually, he will be consumed by it just like his father.

Either way, I will escape. I'll find a way to get far away from the prince and the king. I need to figure out how to stop them. That's what the hero would do. At least, that's what my parents always told me.

CHAPTER SIX

It's been a week since the prince brought me back to Wylan, and I find myself growing more irritated with each day that passes. I have no idea what the Kingdom of Wylan looks like, but the castle walls are covered entirely in mirrors. Everywhere. Not a single wall is without a mirror, which is made even creepier by the fact that they are all covered in black fabric. How do I know they are mirrors if they are covered you may ask. Well, curiosity got the best of me, so I lifted the fabric to see what it was hiding. Behind it, I found a broken mirror, which made me wonder why it was covered in the first place.

Not that I mind them being covered. A memory needles its way into my mind of mirrored glass shattering, my mother's blood pouring from her throat, an evil smile, and cold tentacles climbing up my legs. I shiver, trying to dismiss the thought, and focus back on why I was marching down the hallway to begin with.

Irritation. I'm irritated. The entire time I've been here, there has been a guard assigned to watch my every move, making an escape impossible. Out of the six guards I've had—the same six males who accompanied Prince Dax to bring me here—Asher is the one who irritates me the most.

My anger seems to reach a boiling point and overflow as I march down the hall. Today's shadow follows behind with a cheerful whistle. He's been following me all day. "Asher, you do not have to follow me EVERYWHERE!" His constant happy attitude only feeds my irritation.

"Yes, I do, Little Snow Bunny."

I look over my shoulder to glare as I snap, "Not my name!"

He shrugs and continues to follow me. "I feel the name is fitting. You're a small bunny just flitting around trying not to get caught."

"I have been caught!" I screech.

"Hum... you may have been caught, but I wouldn't say you're trapped."

I ignore him as I throw open the doors to Dax's meeting room. At some point during the last week, I found some courage. I quickly realized Dax wouldn't treat me like his father had. I don't fully understand where my courage came from, but the guards haven't done anything to me either. Which could also be feeding my bravery. Though, some of that courage could be fueled by my fear of not knowing what his plans are for me.

He's not currently in a meeting, only working on paperwork at his desk. His eyes briefly look up before returning to his work. "Good afternoon, Eira. Are you in need of something?"

"I want to leave."

He pauses over his paperwork and looks up to meet my eyes. "You wish to leave." He hesitantly repeats each word as if trying to understand the meaning behind them.

I narrow my eyes at him as I state, "Yes. I want to leave."

His eyes flick to Asher behind me before returning to me. "If you wish to leave the castle, you only need to ask one of my men. I'm sure Ash will gladly guard you as you walk the grounds."

"I do not wish to be guarded! I wish to be free! *I WANT TO LEAVE!*"

He arches an unimpressed brow as he leans back in his chair. "Where would you go? You certainly cannot go back to your kingdom because my father is there. The other kingdoms would not take you in, considering my father controls them as well. Plus, they would dread retaliation for aiding and housing the female who was gifted to the prince by the very king they fear. So tell me, Little Raven. Where would you go?"

"I will not be trapped in this prison!"

He leans forward, his light blue eyes dancing in the light. "Have I chained you?"

"No... but..."

His voice rises over mine. "Have I locked you in your bedroom?"

My cheeks heat. "No."

"Have I forced myself upon you? Have I allowed my men to rape you?"

My voice is meek as I reply, "No."

"Then do tell me, how exactly are you trapped in my kingdom? I have provided you with my protection."

"Your protection means nothing," I sneer.

He shrugs as he leans back again. "It should."

"You are just another villain like your father. You hold just as much responsibility for murdering an entire kingdom as he does," I spit, venom behind each word.

"Eira," Asher whispers urgently from behind me.

Dax's body stiffens as he arches a brow. "Do I? Have you seen me kill anyone?"

"No. But I'm sure you have."

"Eira!" Asher reprimands loudly from behind me, but I pay him no mind. I focus only on the devilish prince in front of me. I can see the rage building behind his gaze, but for some reason it doesn't scare me. Not like his father's gaze did.

"Oh, I have, Little Raven. But I guarantee they deserved it."

I snort. "I doubt that."

His eyes narrow as he says, "You seem to be under the impression that you are the only one my father has hurt on his path to devour the kingdoms. You are a naive child if you think this world is anything but consumed in gray. Are you so enamored by your sense of justice that you believe this world is black and white?"

I stiffen at his words, my gaze narrowing on him. "Right and wrong do exist. That is all. And what could your father possibly do to you? You are his son."

He lets out a humorless laugh as he stands abruptly, causing me to jump. "You think that just because his blood runs through my veins, I was spared his cruelty?" He rips open his shirt, and underneath I see hundreds of scars. Each knife cut leaving a bright pink scar against his creamy skin. There's also a visible handprint scar on his chest. It looks blistered against his skin. "I have felt the cool kiss of his knife as well as the burn of his magic."

He buttons his shirt back up as he looks away. "Do not assume you or the people of these kingdoms are the only ones my father has mutilated. His cruel hands forged me into the man I am. I rule with an obsidian heart because there is no other version of me."

His eyes meet Asher's as he says, "Take her to see the kingdom. Maybe she will understand how the new world works when she sees the amount of damage my father has done."

I look over my shoulder to see Asher's eyes turn sad. "Yes, Your Highness."

My eyes jump back to the prince when he says, "She needs to learn that one must change to fit the world. The world will not change for *anyone*, let alone a naive princess. Adapt or be killed." His eyes flash black before returning to their ice blue. "I've had to adapt because there was no other choice."

"Why are all the mirrors around the castle broken and covered?" I ask, unable to stop the words from tumbling out.

He arches a brow, and a smirk tilts his lips. "Mirrors give my father power. I do not wish for him to have power within my castle."

"What's the point of covering them if they are already broken?"

His smirk disappears, and he says darkly, "Even broken things have power, Eira."

I open my mouth to ask more questions, but Asher grips my shoulder. "Eira, please. You have said enough."

Arching a brow at his use of the word please, I give him a sharp nod before turning back to the prince. "I shall take my leave, Your Highness."

He looks to Asher and orders, "Take a few others with you. There has been activity around the walls."

"Is it wise to take her outside, then?"

He shrugs before turning to face the windows, which allows him a view of the kingdom as well as the large wall surrounding it. "She needs to understand the world we live in now. This is no longer the world she grew up in as a child." He turns to look at me over his shoulder. "It seems her mother kept her in the dark about many things. And my father kept her locked up for too long. If the raven wishes to use her wings and fly, I'll allow it."

He turns back to the windows, heaving out a heavy sigh. "I'm sure she will learn that the outside world will not give her the freedom she seeks. We live in a cage of death and destruction. At least my cage provides comfort and protection." Running a hand through his dark, tufted hair he continues, "Take Kasim and Benedict. They should provide enough protection for you to leave and come back quickly."

Asher steps up beside me as he whines, "Dax, come on. Why do I have to take Kasim?"

Dax smirks at the man beside me. "Because he is the only one I trust to keep the three of you in line and not do something stupid."

Asher's cheeks pinken as he huffs out, "I won't do anything stupid with Eira with me."

"Yes... well, he will be there just to make sure."

Asher groans. "Fine." Turning to me, he gives me a smile and offers me his elbow. "Shall we go?"

I'm not sure what's going on here, but the banter between these two has completely thrown me. Why does the prince allow his subordinates to speak to him that way? It isn't normal to speak to those in lower positions like that.

Narrowing my eyes on Asher, I take his offered elbow anyways. Just because I don't like being here doesn't mean I should be rude. My parents raised me with manners. Right before we exit the room, I hear Dax call out, "Please do not stray too far outside the walls, Ash. I do not want a repeat of what happened last time."

Asher sucks in a breath beside me and looks a bit guilty as he nods. "Understood."

Chapter Seven

On our way out of the castle, we stop to grab Kasim. He follows behind, a deep frown on his face. "This is a stupid idea. Why should we risk our lives for a spoiled princess who doesn't care what happens to us?" he grumbles.

I flinch at his words, and Asher gives my hand a squeeze. Looking over his shoulder, Asher replies, "She doesn't know what the world is like now. Her parents didn't tell her what was going on, and you know Dax's father certainly didn't educate her."

I can feel Kasim glaring at the back of my head, and he huffs out, "Doesn't change the fact she doesn't give a fuck about what happens to us. We risked enough by making the journey to pick her up."

Asher leans down to whisper in my ear, "I promise he normally isn't this grumpy. We lost men on the journey to Arcelia. We were lucky not to have lost anymore on the way back to Wylan."

I arch a brow in question. How is it possible they lost people on the journey to Arcelia? With a sad smile, he says, "You will understand once you see what lies beyond the walls."

As we approach the doors of the towering walls, Kasim yells from behind us, "Open the doors. Weapons at the ready. If you see anything coming our way, you shoot."

Archers are wedged within arrow slits strategically placed through-out the wall. "Yes, sir," echoes around us as the door slowly begins to rise.

I gasp once I'm able to see the other side. Kasim lets out a humorless chuckle as he comes up beside me. "You've seen nothing yet, *Princess.*"

Why is it when he says princess it sounds like poison spilling from his lips. Asher tightens his grip on my arm, and my gaze shifts to see his windblown, chocolate-colored hair moving in the wind. His eyes don't drift to me, though, as he continues to survey the land beyond the wall. "Nothing will happen to you, Eira."

Kasim snorts as he begins walking forward. "Shame. One less spoiled princess in the world would be nice."

I bristle at his words. "Excuse me, who are you calling spoiled? I may be a princess, but that does not mean I'm spoiled."

He looks over his shoulder, arching a brow. "If you say so. Al-though, you're not much of a princess anymore, are you? To be a princess you need a kingdom. Your kingdom was stolen, and your people were killed, so you are a princess of nothing now."

"Kas!" Asher hisses.

He looks to Asher before dropping his gaze back to me. "What, it's the truth isn't it? That's how those fancy titles work."

My eyes narrow on him as I ask, "What is your problem? You don't seem to have this much venom directed toward your prince. He rules over you and has a fancy title, as you so eloquently put it."

He smirks. "Dax may be a prince, but he's a warrior first." He looks me up and down before adding, "It takes more to earn the respect and loyalty of your people than having a fancy title. Remember that when you think you are entitled to something just because your blood reeks of privilege."

As much as I hate his attitude, he does have a point. But I'm not about to give him the satisfaction of agreeing with him. A screeching sound outside the wall makes me jump. I look around, but I don't see anything.

Kasim looks in the direction of the noise, huffs out a sigh, and looks back over his shoulder at Asher and me. "Make sure she doesn't scream. You know that only provokes them."

"Scream? Why would I scream?" I feel my heart quicken at his words.

Asher pats my hand that rests in the crook of his elbow. "I would advise you not to scream, please. If you think you will, please scream into my arm."

My wide eyes met his, but the usual laughter behind his steely blue gaze is missing, replaced with determination. All I can do is nod as I look nervously back out to the barren land of blackness. I suck in a breath when I see a humanoid figure walking oddly in our direction.

I say humanoid because while it may be the shape of a human, it looks nothing like a human. Its skin is gray, and it has white orbs for eyes. Its clothes are torn and dirty. "What is that?" I whisper.

"A death-bringer," Kasim answers darkly.

"Those are the people who have lost their lives and are now nothing but soulless corpses that wander the lands. They do only as the king bids. They kill anything and everything that moves. It's why we have the wall," Asher explains.

"To protect everyone inside," I say breathlessly.

"They normally hunt in groups. We haven't figured out why, but it's best if we don't leave the protection of these walls unless required." Kasim looks back at me, his eyes dark and judgmental. "Our prince left the safety of these walls for you."

My body stiffens as he walks back toward Asher and me. He lifts a hand in the air and yells, "Close the door." His eyes never leave mine as he continues in our direction. Once he is standing right in front of me, he says, "We lost twelve men because we left the protection of the wall... for you. As heartless as you think we may be, those were great men who didn't deserve to lose their lives."

He continues with a sneer, "A spoiled princess who doesn't know what is going on in the world. A naive brat who believes the world is black and white. Who believes herself a hero." He gestures over his shoulder to the wall. "Well, Princess, how are you going to save the world since you think so highly of yourself? Are you going to save the rest of us, so we don't turn into death-bringers? We had to burn the bodies of the twelve men, so they would not turn into those things! Their families have no bodies to mourn!"

"Kas," Asher sighs beside me.

Kasim turns his glare on Asher. "Stop protecting her, Ash! If she thinks us the villains, then let her continue believing so. I don't care if I'm the villain." His eyes shift back to me. "I would rather be a villain than a conceited hero." His eyes narrow and spits out, "Who will mourn the hero princess of nothing when she fails?" With one last disgusted look, he stomps off, heading back to the castle.

I stand stiffly as I stare at the door standing between us and the outside world. Leading directly to where I want to escape. Or was... was wanting to escape. These men are right... I am a naive princess. I didn't ask enough questions, and I certainly did not look into the surrounding kingdoms as much as I should have when the king started taking over. My chest aches when I think over his last words. *Who will mourn the hero princess of nothing?* No one... that's the truth; no one will mourn me because I have no one left. No one who cares for me. No one I love. And no one who loves me...

I'm jerked from my depressing thoughts when Asher pops up in front of me. He levels me with a look and says, "Eira? Eira, pay him no mind. He's taking out his anger over losing soldiers on you."

"He's not wrong, though," I whisper.

Asher shakes his head. "No, he's just angry. It's not your fault that you weren't informed."

"It is, though. I should have asked more questions when I had the chance to get answers, but I didn't. I thought my status as princess would automatically give me those answers."

When he reaches up, I can't help but flinch. His hand stops a few inches from my face before curling into a fist. He looks away from me as he quietly says, "Please don't cry."

I didn't realize I was crying until I reached up to touch my face. My vision blurs as the tears start to fall faster. I let out a hiccupped laugh. "I'm so pathetic. A princess of nothing, just like Kasim said."

Asher straightens and steps closer, wrapping his arms around me. He pulls me into his chest, just holding me close. His hold isn't tight, which allows me the ability to break away if needed. "Just because we are villains does not mean we are without a heart. Kasim is angry, and he feels the loss of the men he trained for years. He said many things out of anger, whether true or not."

"He does not like me," I mutter.

"He doesn't like most people, to be honest." He sighs. "I like you more when you are feisty and angry."

I let out a watery laugh and say, "You mean to say you like Snow Bunny me."

He laughs softly. "She is my favorite." He gives me a soft squeeze before pulling away. "Let's head back to the castle. I'm sure we can find some way to entertain you," he teases.

I wipe my face as I peer up at him. "I did not realize it was your job to entertain me."

He shrugs and offers me his elbow again. "I'm your guard for the day. My job is to take care of you."

I can't stop the smile that pulls at my lips as I slip my hand through to hold his forearm. I may have hated his happy attitude before, but right now, it's the only thing drawing me out of my depressive mood. I need to be more open-minded while here. It's time to learn everything I possibly can because I won't stop until I get my kingdom back.

I need to do whatever is necessary. Which means I need to learn from the villains. It will take a villain to defeat another. I'm beginning to realize the heroes I grew up with bowed to villains instead of fighting them.

CHAPTER

EIGHT

DAX

From the first moment I laid eyes on her, I knew she was mine. An ache I had never felt before grew in my chest as her bright sapphire eyes looked up at me. I saw the strength behind those eyes. The satisfaction I felt when I realized my father had not broken her made me force a frown on my face. Because the smile that tried to crawl across my lips would not do in front of my father. He would see me beaten for such a cheerful smile.

I know Eira hates my guts as much as she hates my father, but that doesn't lessen the need I feel for her to be mine. A little raven trapped within a gilded cage of my own making. I can't think of a better analogy than that. Better to be trapped in a gilded cage than the cold, dank place I'm sure my father held her in.

When Ash had called her a snow bunny, I had to bite my lip to avoid laughing. She looked as if she wished to punch him in the face for uttering a name such as that. To be honest, I would have happily taken a beating from my father to watch that happen. I'm sure Ash would have let her get a hit in too. The man loves bloodshed, whether it be his or a prisoner's. It's why he is so good at interrogation; he doesn't mind the blood spatter.

I smirk as I think over the last week and how her face contorted every time he was assigned as her guard. Her eyes seem to glow with anger each time he calls her a snow bunny. It's amusing if I'm honest. It makes the long days bearable and this cold castle feel a bit warmer.

I had started to wonder when she would finally confront me about leaving the castle, but I was not expecting her to be bold enough to fling open my doors the way she did. To be honest, it took me off guard at first. To see her fury and meet my gaze unflinchingly. It takes courage to confront someone you believe to be a villain. Even more so when the villain is the son of an even greater villain.

Thinking about my father has me huffing out a heavy sigh and rubbing at the handprint branded across my chest. I did not expect her words to burn as deeply as my father's hand. Though a woman filled with that much fire is sure to burn any man who dares to cross her path. Even a cold-hearted man like me.

"She did not mean her words, Dax."

Jolted out of my thoughts, I peer over my shoulder to find Reverie hiding in the corner. Always wrapped in shadows. His dark skin allows such grace, but I believe Rev is more comfortable watching from the shadows and dark spaces of the castle. I'm sure my other men could hide within the shadows as well, but the man in front of me appears to be darkness incarnate. Turning away from him and back toward the window, I stare out at the wasteland that is my kingdom. "She meant them, Rev. She doesn't seem like a woman who says things she does not mean."

He steps out of the corner and away from the darkness. I can hear his footsteps, which means he wishes for me to hear him as he comes to stand beside me. My silent killer. A true assassin within my ranks. "She is a child. Her words are those of a naive princess who does not know any better."

I huff out a laugh. "She is anything but a child. Naive? Yes, but that is her parents' fault for not providing her with the proper education for a queen-to-be. My father certainly would not have educated her while she was his prisoner. She was his toy to play with and break, nothing more."

Groaning, I pinch the bridge of my nose, trying to stave off the headache I can feel behind my eyes. Rev stands closer, bumping his shoulder into mine. "She seems to stave off your headaches, and your darkness seems to calm when she is around."

Sighing, I take a seat on my chair. Lounging back, I close my eyes. "Yes, it does seem like she soothes the turbulence within my mind. Not that her opinion of me would change with that knowledge. I believe she would purposefully stay away if she were aware."

I feel him lean against the desk beside me. "You think she is that vindictive and cunning?"

"I think her hatred of me is that potent," I point out. "She would do it just to spite me, knowing that it would hurt me in doing so."

He hums thoughtfully as we settle into a comfortable silence. It's a few minutes before Rev huffs out a sigh and asks, "When do you think your father will visit to check on his pet?"

"It will not take long," I say with a grunt. Truthfully, I'm surprised he hasn't already visited to check up on Eira. I thought he would have shown up here at least a day or so ago. Which means he will be arriving here in the next few days. I groan as I realize this means I should warn her of his presence.

As if reading my thoughts, Rev asks, "Do you plan to warn her that he will be coming here soon?"

My brows pinch, and the pain behind my eyes increases. My voice sounds strained as I reply, "I am still thinking about it."

He laughs. "I did not think it would be much of a debate, Dax."

I crack one eye open to glare at him. "It seems my obsidian heart beats after all. An odd feeling after all these years if I'm honest."

He winces, hearing my words for what they truly mean. I may not be as cruel as my father, but I am still cruel, nonetheless. To rule the required way, emotions must be stripped away. A cruel prince feels nothing but anger and malice. Though, it seems a certain woman is starting to change that.

"She will become a weakness," he says quietly.

My eye falls closed again. "Then it is good I have six men by my side who I trust with my life."

He grunts before saying, "Ash seems enamored by her."

I shrug. "He has always been the cheerful one. Maybe his lively attitude will allow her to trust the rest of us."

His voice is filled with surprise as he asks, "Us?"

"Can you not feel it, brother?"

Confusion laces his words as he says, "Feel what?"

A grin spreads across my face as I reply, "She's ours."

Chapter Nine

Eira

I don't think I should feel as comfortable as I do here in Wylan. But I do. It feels as if a lifetime has passed since I was brought here, but it's only been two weeks. I still have a constant rotation of guards, always the same six males the prince brought with him to Arcelia.

Kasim still irritates me every time he has guard duty. He either silently glares at me or will not shut up about how spoiled of a princess I am. I refuse to give him the satisfaction of knowing that his attitude bothers me or that his words cut deeper than the scars across my skin. He is nothing but a grump, which is my new nickname for him, Grumpy Man.

Asher has slowly become my favorite to have guard me. He always has a smile on his face and appears to be happy more often than not. He is the much-needed sunshine on my dark days, and I look forward to the days he is my guard.

I have not had the chance to learn much about Alair other than that he often jokes with the passing guards. He's much like Asher in that way. He tries to make me laugh when we are together, and he focuses more on me than himself. Although, his dimples are adorable when he laughs, so I suppose I have learned one thing about him.

Branimir is quiet and usually sports pink cheeks around me. His freckles stand out against his bright cheeks when he blushes. I have a feeling he doesn't spend much time around women. When he worries he's too bold with his questions, his ears turn as red as his hair. He often has to brush it back as it tends to fall into his face when he ducks my gaze.

Reverie usually stays in the shadows when it's his turn to guard me. Allowing me to roam the hallways and rooms freely. I cannot count how many times he has scared me by popping out of the shadows. He seems so comfortable in the shadows that he has become one with the darkness itself.

Today, my guard is Benidict. *Sigh*. He is so beautiful. He has long platinum-blond hair and dark brown orbs that remind me of a mythical being rather than a soldier. He often takes me to the library where I attempt to learn everything I can about the kingdoms. I'm not sure how I'm going to read the thousands of books the prince has managed to procure, but I am going to do my best.

We are quietly walking down the hallway toward the library as usual when I can no longer stand the silence. "So, Benedict..."

"You can call me Bene."

I smile as I nod. "Okay. So... Bene, how long have you known the prince?"

"Dax? Hum... I've known him since we were children. The seven of us grew up together."

My brows knit as I ask, "Is everyone around here always so informal with the prince's title?"

Bene laughs and explains, "The seven of us call each other by name, considering how long we have known one another. We only use titles when necessary." His eyes glitter with amusement as he says, "He would not mind if you called him Dax instead of prince."

I bite my lip as I debate his words. With a huff, I say, "It feels weird to call him Dax. I feel like I should call him prince. It's what I was taught."

Bene shrugs and holds open the door for me. "Much of what we were taught is no longer relevant in the world we live in now. You don't have to be as formal with us."

I nod as I make my way through the library and head to a section I haven't had the chance to look at yet. Running my fingers along the dusty spines, I blow off the dust, so I can see the titles.

I jump, letting out a screech of fright when a loud noise erupts from behind me. I look back to find Bene rubbing his nose. My eyes widen. "What the hell kind of noise was that?"

He looks up at me, confused, then looks around the library before turning back to me with an arched brow. "It was just a sneeze. These books are super dusty; they've haven't been touched in a while."

I shake my head as I argue, "That was *NOT* a normal sneeze. It sounded as if a demon just left your body!"

He snorts. "I have never had my sneeze compared to a demon leaving my body before."

Turning back to the rows of books, I huff out, "Well, someone should have. That sneeze would frighten children."

He chuckles as he trails behind me. "I will keep that in mind if I ever need to frighten children."

I feel my cheeks heat as I nod. "You do that."

"Are you looking for anything specific, Eira? I can help if you would like."

"Really?"

He seems confused by my question. "Yes? Do you not want my help?"

I almost drop the books in my arms as I spin toward him, shaking my head. "No, that is not what I meant. I only... I just thought you may not want to help the woman who thinks of the prince as a villain."

"Why would I not want to help you? If I don't help you that would only reinforce your views of us were correct, would it not?"

My eyes lower and trace one of the many designs on the floor. "I suppose," I whisper.

He lowers himself enough to catch my eyes with his. "Have you ever thought that maybe villains are just misunderstood?"

My brows furrow. "What do you mean?"

Placing a finger under my chin, he raises my face to meet his gaze. With a soft smile, he says, "Everyone always views villains as evil beings. But did you ever think that maybe the villains just live by a different set of morals? Maybe my morals don't adhere to those of a hero, but that doesn't mean I don't have any. So am I really the villain, or do I just not fit the standards the heroes wish for me to adhere to?"

I'm about to reply, but he places a finger over my lips. "I am not saying we aren't villains; I am only saying we may not be as bad as you believe us to be." He pulls away, taking a step back. "Continue your search, Eira. I'll leave you to your thoughts."

I watch him take another step back before turning to head in the direction of the sitting area. I stand frozen as I try to process his words. Is he right? He does have a point. Are my views on heroes and villains skewed because of what I was taught? Is there a definitive line between good and evil, or is there a blurred area of good intentions?

I know true good and true evil exist, but what fills the space between the two? Do Dax and his men live in the space between?

CHAPTER TEN

"The king will be here within the next few hours," a deep voice says from the doorway. I look up from the book I'm reading and find Dax in the entrance to the library.

Bene is sitting beside me with his own book and looks up with a huff. "I am surprised it took him this long to visit." He sets down the book he was reading and stands, hesitantly turning to hold out a hand to me. "We should get you ready for the king's arrival."

I arch a brow as I set my book aside, then take his offered hand. "What do you mean?"

Bene's eyes dart to Dax before landing back on me. He sighs before saying, "You must look and act the part of the prince's toy while he's here. The king has certain expectations, and how we've treated you here, and allowed you to do certain things, is not even in the realm of what the king would find suitable."

My eyes shift to Dax, and I allow his name to slip from my lips. "Dax? He won't take me back with him, will he?"

His eyes widen in surprise for a moment before his expression turns neutral again. "No, he will not be taking you back with him."

My grip on Bene's hand tightens as I quietly ask, "You promise?"

He arches a brow and smirks. "I said you were under my protection, did I not?"

Taking a deep breath, I nod. "Yes."

He crosses his arms over his chest as Bene and I make our way over to him. "I suppose this means you'll have to trust the villain."

My eyes meet his bright blue ones as I nod. "I suppose it does. I do hope if you plan to betray me, you will kill me before handing me back over to him."

Dax offers me his elbow as he gives me a small smile. "I have no reason to betray you." I slip my hand through the crook of his arm as he lowers his voice to a whisper. "If I were planning to kill you, I would have done it the day we met. I would not have allowed my men to be beguiled by your beauty."

My eyes widen at his words. "Beguile your men, huh?"

He chuckles as he and Bene usher me down the hallway. "Yes, beguile my men. Whether you believe it or not, Little Raven, you hold more power than you think. I know you have put Asher under a spell for sure."

I gasp at his accusatory words. "I am not a witch! I have put no one under a spell."

"You do not have to be a witch to put my men under a spell, Little Raven. You cannot convince me you haven't enchanted Asher. He does not shut up about you. He constantly asks me to be your permanent guard." He gives me a wink before he adds, "The only reason I have declined is because he is amazing with the new recruits. He sets them at ease during training."

My cheeks heat as Bene opens the door to my room before releasing my hand. Stepping aside to guard the door, he says, "I'll wait outside to take you to the great hall to receive the king."

Dax unwinds my hand from his arm. "I set out an outfit for you. Forgive the lack of material, but it is what my father will expect to see you wearing. Once he leaves, you may return and change."

I peer into the room to find the outfit laid out on the bed. He's right, there isn't much material to it. It will cover my breasts, but the long slits up the sides will leave my legs exposed and barely cover my vagina. I suppose if his father expects Dax and his men to treat me the way he and his men did, they will need easy access.

I shiver at the memories. Dax gives my hand a squeeze before releasing it. "Are you alright, Eira?"

Jerking myself out of those nightmares, I give him a smile. "Of course. Thank you for the clothes."

He watches me for a moment, his eyes narrowing on my face, then he looks at the outfit laid out for me. When he turns back, his eyes are black as night. "He did not clothe you, did he?"

The thought of lying to him crosses my mind, but it feels wrong to do so, considering the freedom he has given me here. Biting my lip, I shake my head. "No," I say softly.

His voice shakes as he asks, "His men... he allowed his men to visit you?"

I feel myself shrinking away from the anger that radiates off him. "Yes."

With a stiff nod, he says, "I must take my leave now. I will see you in the great hall."

I watch him march off, swirls of darkness trailing behind, and I jump when Bene speaks quietly. "Dax has lines he *will not* cross, and his father crosses many of them."

"Is that why he left so quickly?"

Bene nods. "Dax has great control over the darkness. Better control than his father has. It helps that the six of us hold a piece of it as well, so it is not as overwhelming."

My eyes widen. "You each hold a piece of the darkness?"

He nods as he points to his chest. The same spot where Dax has a handprint scar. "His father branded him with a curse. It slowly eats at your soul until there isn't much of you left. We each hold a piece for Dax, so his soul won't be torn apart like his father's."

I point at my eyes as I ask, "Is that why his eyes sometimes turn black?"

He nods. "The darkness thrives on dark emotions. Anger. Grief. Envy. Things like that. And when the emotions become too much, the darkness will try to overwhelm him. He walked away because he did not wish to hurt you."

I look in the direction Dax left before I turn back to Bene. "Are you guys safe? Am I safe to be around all of you?"

He laughs. "We are the safest people in all the kingdoms for you to be around."

"How do you figure?"

He smiles and takes a step closer, invading my space. Reaching up, he brushes a thumb across my lips as he replies, "You aren't ready to hear the answer to that, Darling."

"What... what do you mean?" I ask breathlessly as I watch his eyes bleed to black like ink. Those ebony pits of his drawing me in while he stares at me.

"The truth would make you run." He leans closer until his lips are a hair's breadth away from mine. "And that would be dangerous for you."

"Why is that?" I whisper.

His tongue darts across my lips before he replies, "I wouldn't be able to control the darkness." He shifts, so his lips caress my ear, making me shiver. "It loves a good chase, Darling. I'm sure Ash would love to hunt his little snow bunny."

Heat builds in my stomach as my breathing becomes choppy. I lick my lips and say, "Then I'll make sure not to run."

With a laugh, he pulls away, backing up to stand next to the door again. He gives me a wink and teases, "Unless you want to be caught."

With a stiff nod, I scurry into my room, slamming the door behind me. I take a deep breath and fall back against the door, fanning my face when I feel my cheeks burn. I've never been this flustered over a man before. Although, the men I have spent most of my days with were the king's men.

None of the men I've met have as much charm as these males do. Thumping my head against the door, I sigh. Even though Kasim infuriates me, he is still attractive. Taking a few more deep breaths in and out, I push away from the door and begin to undress, knowing I will have to trust these men to protect me in the presence of the king.

I could see the truth in Dax's eyes when he said he would protect me. But that doesn't stop my heart from pounding with fear at the thought of having to return to that awful place I once loved so much. The fear of being helpless and back at that man's mercy causes my stomach to flip. I shake myself to banish those thoughts and feelings.

I know one thing for sure. I would steal a sword and kill myself before I ever allowed the king's hands on me again.

CHAPTER ELEVEN

"Hello, Little Snowflake," I hear a voice boom across the great hall, making me flinch.

Bene stands beside me, and he stiffens at the king's greeting. His hand tightens on mine, which rests on his forearm. I take a deep breath, trying to calm my racing heart. I have to remind myself that Bene is here with me; he won't let the king do anything. Not wanting to cause any issues, I return his greeting. "Hello."

His eyes are their normal mirrored black, and I've always thought it an odd color. More so now, since I know the guys' eyes change from normal to black and then back again. Has the king lost all humanity?

He hums as he takes in his son. "She seems docile. Did you break her in?"

Dax shrugs as his eyes shift to me briefly before returning to his father. "I clipped her wings. An illusion of freedom, but she is still trapped within my cage." He gives his father a dark smile as he says, "If she tries to escape, she can flit about, but clipped wings can only get you so far."

The king grins maliciously. "Clipped wings indeed. I do hope she has been fun to play with." I shiver when he says *play* because I know what he means by that. The swirls of black smoke floating around him seem to grow erratic. "I have missed your tears, Little Snowflake. Maybe I should have some fun while I visit."

There's a cacophony of growls from the males in the room. My eyes widen when I see that all of their eyes have changed to black. Reverie steps out of the darkness as he glares at the king. His eyes are completely black and look otherworldly with his dark skin.

Kasim looks like a wild animal as he snarls in the king's direction with inky eyes. Branimir stands beside him, glaring as well but staying quiet. His black eyes contrast against his reddened cheeks and fiery hair.

Asher comes to stand to my other side, and Bene's grip on me tightens. I look at Asher first to find my normally happy guard has turned serious as he scowls in the king's direction. His hand comes up to brush against my back as if he would sweep me away if need be.

Alair flanks Dax, both shifting to reveal their swords. With eyes dark as night, Dax's voice rumbles across the room, "*We* do not share."

The king laughs. "I see. Well, then I would love a demonstration at least." His eyes narrow on his son as he continues, "It's the least you can do, considering I gifted you with my toy."

Dax's eyes shift to me briefly before darting back to his father. "Very well. But you will be waiting outside the chamber. Your eyes will *never* see her naked body again. She's *mine.*"

The way he growls *mine* sends a shiver down my spine. I want to say that whatever he has planned isn't going to happen, but I know this situation won't end well if I disagree with the prince in front of his father.

The king gives a sharp nod. "Very well. Let's have some fun. If I'm not able to participate, I wish to get this done, so I may return home to play with my other toys."

Dax nods and shoots Bene a look. "Take her to the guest bed chamber."

Bene ushers me ahead of the others, and I almost miss the king saying, "I see you have covered the mirrors. Such a shame."

"Mirrors do not have a place in my castle, Father. I certainly do not want the being within your mirrors checking up on me or trying to control me," Dax grumbles.

The being? Is he talking about the tentacles that come out of the mirror? The king chuckles. "Nothing controls me, son. Best you remember that."

I hear Dax grunt behind me, and we continue down the hallway. I wish I could argue against what they are planning. But I also have a lot of questions. I suppose I can wait till we are behind closed doors again to give Dax a piece of my mind. Though, considering all their eyes are engulfed in black, I may lose my nerve.

My mouth is dry, but I manage to whisper, "So... what's the plan here?"

Asher's gravelly voice sounds from right behind me. "We are going to make the king believe we are torturing you."

"Do I want to know how you guys plan to do that?"

His eyes flash back to their normal light blue before black consumes them once more. He grins. "Do you really want to know, Snow bunny?"

The look he sends me before his eyes shift back to black makes me want to say no. No, I do not want to know because it will just make me want to run.

As if reading my mind, Bene lowers to whisper in my ear, "Do run, Darling. We would love a good chase. The darkness is *hungry*." The way he growls hungry makes heat pool low in my belly.

Ash opens the door to the bed chamber with a flourish before heading in. I jump when I hear the door slam shut behind me. Looking over my shoulder, I see Dax bathed in swirls of dark shadows. Admittedly, he doesn't look scary like his father does; he looks like a hungry beast. And I'm his prey. Pulling my hand away from Bene, I turn to face Dax.

The others fan out around the room. Gathering every bit of courage I can, I manage to ask, "So what is the plan, Dax?"

The sound that comes from him is almost like a purr. Did he seriously purr just because I said his name? He takes a step toward me, and I retreat a step. He shoots me a wicked smile as he takes another step forward, and I do the same but back. We continue this dance until my legs hit the foot of the bed.

I quickly glance over my shoulder then back to find him standing right in front of me. I gasp when I see the metallic glint of a knife. He holds it out in front of him, testing the sharpness of the tip. When his eyes meet mine, all I see is my reflection in those deep ebony pits.

"I'm going to make each of those scars mine. Each cut will remind you of me. *Only* me," he says, pushing me down, so I fall onto my back on the bed.

"Are you serious?" My voice sounds less like a question and more like a breathy gasp. Damn.

He smirks as he lifts the blade. "Do I look serious to you?"

He does in fact look serious. He also looks like he is going to enjoy this way too much and, considering the heat pooling in my abdomen, I think I will too. I can already feel my thin underwear getting wet.

Even though my body betrays me, my mind won't. "You hold no power over me." Though these men are completely different than my previous sexual encounters. They are different than the king and his disgusting guards. Different from the smooth, mirrored tentacles that forced me to climax.

He grins and taunts, "Are you sure about that, Little Raven?"

"Yes," I state rather unconvincingly. My body wants these men, and my mind can no longer fight that it does too. I don't hate them like I do the king and his guards, and my body knows it.

"I'm going to have fun testing that." He turns to Branimir and orders, "Mir, hold her arm."

Without argument, Branimir steps up to my right. He pulls me up toward the head of the bed and clamps down on my wrist, pinning it above my head. I don't have time to fight because Dax continues issuing orders, immediately saying, "Bene, grab her other arm."

He does the same, holding my left wrist, so both of my arms are pinned over my head. Dax points the knife at Alair. "Hold her leg; I'll need them spread far apart for what I have planned." He points his knife to Reverie next. "Rev, hold her other leg."

Alair does as he is told, holding down my right leg as Rev holds my left. They spread my legs apart making me feel like a starfish.

My eyes go wide when I realize I am completely powerless and vulnerable in this position. "Dax! Dax, what are you doing?"

He smirks at me. "I'm going to make you hurt so good, Little Raven. I'll make sure you leave here so thoroughly satisfied that you will be as obsessed with us as we are with you."

"All of you couldn't possibly be obsessed with me," I insist.

He clicks his tongue and slips the tip of the knife under my clothes. "Then you haven't been paying enough attention." He turns to Asher as he says, "Ash, by her head."

Ash climbs onto the bed, and his knees frame my head. "Can't have you looking away, Snow Bunny."

I screech when I feel the knife slice through my clothes, leaving me completely bare except for my underwear. He taps the blade right below my belly button. "Seems I have a lot of scars to mark as my own, Little Raven."

He slides the knife under the sides of my panties, cutting them off me and letting out a hiss when I'm completely bared before the seven of them. I look up to see him staring intently at my center. He licks his lips before meeting my gaze. "You're soaked. You're dripping for us already. I wonder what you taste like. Do you taste as sweet as you smell?" He groans and sucks on his bottom lip. "It's a shame I already offered Kas the pleasure of tasting that hot sex of yours." He turns to Kas and growls, "You better enjoy it."

I watch as Kas crawls onto the bed, lowering himself, so his face is level with my sex. He gives me a devilish grin as his hot breath brushes my sensitive skin. "I'm starving." But before he lowers to my center, he licks a trail up my thigh. I feel something cool touch my skin before the warmth of his tongue banishes the chill. I catch a glimpse of metal in the middle of his tongue before it vanishes back into his mouth.

"Your skin tastes sweet. I wonder if your cunt will taste sweeter."

"What's that on your tongue?" I ask a bit breathlessly.

He smirks. "What, this?" He sticks out his tongue, allowing me to see it once more. The metal clicks against his teeth as he folds his tongue, so I can see that the metal bar goes all the way through.

"Yes."

"It's a piercing, Princess. Worth the pain to have a woman squirming and screaming as I eat her cunt."

His crass words make me want to say something in return, but my body feels hot and needy, and my brain isn't functioning properly. I'm overwhelmed by the sensations forced upon me by these men. The moment Kas's tongue licks up my center, Dax slices the knife across one of my scars. The combination of the sting of pain from the knife, and the pleasure of Kas's tongue has me wriggling and squirming, but I can't move.

"What does she taste like?" Dax asks and groans.

Kas sucks on my center before licking me from entrance to my clit. "So fucking sweet. The most delicious dessert I've ever had." A moan slips from my lips as Kas spears me with his tongue at the same time Dax makes another cut on my skin. Kas's tongue piercing is hitting places I didn't even know were pleasurable. Each slow stroke of torture has heat building in my abdomen with no relief.

Dax quickens the pace of each slice as Kas slips his tongue from my center, and I let out a screech of irritation. Dax laughs and teases, "Seems you are enjoying yourself, Little Raven."

I'm panting as I open my eyes, which I didn't realize I had closed. I'm greeted by Asher's heated gaze as he looks down at me. He licks his lips while he admires my body. "I want to touch you. I want to taste you. You smell delicious."

I look down to see my abdomen covered in shallow cuts, just deep enough to have blood bubbling to the surface. My eyes shift to Ash again, and he snarls, "I'm touching you."

He reaches out and uses my blood to paint my body before moving his palms to massage my breasts. He pinches my nipples, and I let out a moan. Ash slips a blood covered finger into his mouth, licking it off with a groan. I can feel his cock growing hard where it rests against the top of my head. "You taste like an apple tart."

When Kas removes his tongue and replaces it with a finger, I let out a scream. He begins pumping wildly as he sucks on my clit. The cuts Dax is making against my skin turn erratic as the room fills with growls.

The need to come is overwhelming, and I feel moisture gathering at the corners of my eyes. I've never felt so much pleasure and pain. I'm panting as I grind against Kas's face. I feel the knees beside my head disappear, and I open my eyes to find Ash's face right in front of mine.

He watches as the moisture in my eyes builds, till they slide down my cheeks. With bloodied fingers, he grips my chin, turning it as he lowers his face. I feel his tongue on the side of my temple, licking up to the corner of my eye.

He hums. "Her tears are deliciously sweet too. I want more. I need more." He licks the other side of my face before he stares intently, waiting for more tears of pleasure to fall.

Dax's dark voice vibrates the room as he says, "Then you shall have more."

Kas hums against my clit, and I cry out. He slips another finger inside me and begins to curl them, so they hit that perfect spot each time. My fingers curl into fists as tears stream down my face.

"Scream for us, Little Raven," he growls. "Sing for Kas. Let him know how much you love him fucking your soaking sex with his fingers."

When Kas adds another finger, my back bows off the bed, and my pleasure crescendos to a height I've never felt before. He continues to suck my clit with each pump of his fingers. Suddenly, Kas bites down on my sensitive nub, and my vision compresses into pinpricks before I erupt.

I scream as my body shatters with pleasure. Kas continues to fuck me with his fingers through it all, making my orgasm last longer. I sob as my pleasure continues to grow. Kas, not caring, continues until my body fractures once more before melding with the mattress. I'm completely spent from the overwhelming sensations.

Kas takes one last lick up my center, the cold metal of his tongue ring gliding across my sensitive flesh, making me whine from over-stimulation. I look down with blurry eyes to find his black eyes on me. He lifts just enough, so I can see his mouth and chin are soaked with my release. He lifts a hand, wiping his face before giving me a dark smile. His eyes track the movement of my rapid breathing.

His voice is gruff as his eyes meet mine. "I'm still starving, Princess."

Not wanting to give away how that *epic* orgasm made me like him a little more, I put as much venom behind my words as possible when I narrow my eyes and huff out, "You're *still* not my favorite person today, Kas." Damn that didn't come out right.

He shrugs as he sits back on his heels with a cocky smirk. "I'm not your favorite person on any day, Princess. Doesn't change the fact that I made you come on my face. Twice."

I thump my head back down on the bed. "I hate you!"

"Hate you too, Princess."

A knock on the door makes me flinch; I forgot we had an audience. "Her screams were quite delicious boys. I appreciate the show, but I must be on my way. Hearing her screams makes me hunger for my toys back home."

Silence settles around us as we listen to the king's retreating foot-steps. The quiet becomes a bit suffocating, so I ask awkwardly, "Can I change now? Although maybe I should ask if I'm allowed to get dressed, considering you cut my outfit off?"

Dax chuckles, and he offers me a hand. The hands holding me down release, and I reach for his offered hand. "Why don't you enjoy a bath as well. I'll make sure one of the men brings up some balm for your cuts."

He pulls me to stand, and I peer down at myself to find that *every* cut the king had previously made has now been reopened by Dax. I nod as my eyes meet his. "I would appreciate that."

He presses a kiss to my knuckles before releasing them. With a nod to the door, he says, "Off you go, Little Raven."

It takes every ounce of self-control I possess not to run out of that room. I don't know if what Bene said is true, but I don't want to chance it. The last thing I need is for them to chase me around the castle while I'm naked because I triggered their darkness to take over.

I also can't forget that these men are still the villains. Mild compared to the king maybe, but villains, nonetheless. Still, they are the enemy, and the enemy of my enemy is my friend. Right?

Why is it getting harder to say that and even harder to believe it? It's beginning to taste a lot like a lie.

Chapter Twelve

Dax

A few weeks have passed since my father's visit, and I've noticed how Eira looks at the others. She watches us with hunger in her eyes but refuses to satiate it. I even catch her looking at Kas with lust filled eyes, which makes me grin, considering how much they appear to hate each other. I've heard that hate sex is the best, though. When you are always surrounded by men, sex seems to be the only thing that's talked about. Though I'm surrounded by warriors who spend most of their days fighting, and because we don't have an abundance of women, things tend to get a little... hard.

If I said a burst of jealousy didn't spark within me when I saw her mahogany eyes raking over my men, it would be a lie. Well, the six men I'm soul bound to. Though Ash, Kas, Rev, Alair, Bene, and Mir are mine to lead and command. My brothers. Soul bound until our dying breaths because of the curse. But also because of the battles we have fought. It's hard not to bond with a man you spend every waking moment of the day with, let alone six.

I see the way they look at her, want and hunger burning behind their eyes. Though I feel the need to claim her as mine and mine alone. But I know she is theirs as well. The only one I've spoken to about this is Rev, and even he seemed skeptical about the connection I swear we have with her. Soon they will realize that she belongs to us just as much as we belong to her. I am a possessive bastard, so she will only ever belong to us. No one else.

Her dark eyes are focused on me as my soldiers' spar around us. Her eyes never leave mine as I walk between the bodies, making my way over to her. As I weave between the men, I hold her gaze. Like a game of cat and mouse, or better yet, a dangerous snake that wishes to ensnare a flightless raven.

Ash is working to correct the newer soldiers' forms, while Kas glares from the sidelines. Alair and Bene watch the surrounding area, continuously scanning for threats as they were trained to do. Ensuring we have no soldiers who belong to my father within our ranks. Rev and Mir keep their eyes on me as I walk over to Eira, always making sure I'm not attacked by a rogue that has managed to slip through the watchful eyes of Alair and Bene.

I know what Eira thinks of me. She believes me to be a villain, a horrid prince who kills without mercy. Part of that may be true. I do kill my enemies without mercy. My father is cruel and ruthless in his rule, which in turn made me savage because it was the only way to survive. I kill because it is required of me. This is a wicked world we live in. I am far less sadistic than my father, so she should take my cruelty for what it is. Safety from those who would wish to do much worse than I.

I protect what is mine. She will learn that lesson soon. So until then, I will continue my game. A game to hunt and capture the bird. My little raven. I smirk as I notice her eyes continue to track me. "What are you doing, Little Raven?"

She arches a brow. "Why do you insist on calling me that?"

I point at her hair and say, "Your hair is as dark as a raven's wings. It even has magic that looks as if it changes color when the light shines just right. Plus, I find that you are a bird trying to spread her wings to fly."

She rolls her eyes. "Just because I let your friend fuck me with his fingers and you replaced his scars with your own, doesn't mean we are friends. We are not even acquaintances. Do not give me a pet name as if we are such things. As if you enjoy my company."

I can see she struggles with each word she forces out. She doesn't believe what she's saying but feels as if she should say it anyway. I laugh. "Oh, I enjoy your company very much. I would even go as far as to say that my men also enjoy your company. I did say that you have beguiled them."

Her eyes narrow on me. "I have not beguiled your men. Also, I do not care what you or your men think of me."

"I believe that to be a lie, Little Raven."

She lets out a frustrated screech and runs at me. Rev and Mir stand, ready to rush in my direction until I hold up a hand to stop them. I allow her to jump at me as I throw my weight backward, then let myself fall while I grin at her.

She bares her teeth at me as something sharp and cold is pressed against my throat. I assume it's the dagger she has been hiding this whole time. I knew she had it. The others wanted to take it from her, but I knew she only felt at ease in the castle because she had a weapon. Though, for her to go so far as to hold it to my neck... Well, it seems my little raven has talons. Seems she's a bit frazzled as well if the wild look in her eyes is any indication. She feels things she doesn't want to. She's beginning to care, and that terrifies her.

She snarls and snaps, "Why are you smiling when I have a blade to your throat?"

"Do you think this is the first time someone has held a blade to my throat?" I chuckle and ask, "Do you plan to kill me, Little Raven?"

Her eyes narrow as she growls out, "I have a knife to your neck, Dax. Are you not going to beg for your life?"

She's trying really hard to grasp for her anger, but I see the hesitation behind those mahogany eyes. While holding her gaze, I retort, "I do not beg for much in this life, let alone my life. I've learned a hard lesson in begging, my Little Raven, and I learned it well." I arch a brow as I continue, "So I will not beg. I will not beg for the lives of my people. Lives are lost every day, and that is out of my control. If my life is worth that much to you, then you may take it if you wish. I am a villain after all."

"Such a brave prince," she scoffs. "What would you beg for?"

I don't hesitate to answer. "I would beg for the lives of my men."

She looks up briefly to take in the hundreds of men around us. Her eyes meet mine again as she questions in confusion, "Your men?"

I can feel the edge of the dagger digging deeper into my skin when I swallow. "Yes. I would beg for Asher, Kasim, Reverie, Alair, Benedict, and Branimir's lives. I would beg until my very last breath." And I would. I don't think love is the word I would use for them, but we have a brotherhood and a bond I would kill for. That I would die for.

Her gaze turns curious as she asks, "Is there anyone else you would beg for?"

Why would she ask that? An odd question after what I've revealed. I'm not sure if I want to say more. My eyes narrow as I reply, "You wouldn't believe me if I said."

She presses down on the dagger as she insists, "Try me."

I wince at the sharp bite of the blade against my throat, then huff out a sigh and say, "You."

Her eyes widen with disbelief. "Me?"

Keeping my expression neutral, I say, "You should kiss your true love. I've been told that true love's kiss solves everything." I'm not sure where that came from, but I already said it, so I may as well go with it. I don't think for one moment she will go through with it, but it is fun to tease with her.

Her eyes turn playful, and her grip on the dagger wavers. "And who is my true love? Or would it be loves, considering you said you would share with them? A villainous prince and his men as my true loves?"

My eyes do not waver from hers as I reply, "Yes." Before she has time to react, I slam my lips to hers. I have to hold back a moan at how good she tastes. I wanted to taste her so badly when I ran my knife across her skin earlier. I feel the cold steel slowly slip away from my neck, then hear the thump of the dagger hitting the earth beside us before she reaches out to run her fingers through my hair.

I groan when her grip tightens, and she pulls me closer. I can't help the tilt of my lips as I deepen the kiss. Fuck doe-eyed princes, white steeds, and happy-ever-afters. I'd kill for this woman. I would watch the kingdoms fall and laugh while they burned so long as she is by my side.

A villain is a misunderstood hero, and a hero is a glorified villain. I suppose it depends on who is telling the story. I may be the villain to many throughout this kingdom, but I'll gladly take on that role if it means the ones I care about will be safe.

I'm left panting when the kiss ends, and I look into her eyes. She looks confused and slightly horrified. My hand slips up between us, and I cup her cheek, my thumb brushing across her bottom lip. "If you need me to be the villain in your story, I do not mind. But I need you to understand that once you are mine, that is it. I shall be a sword for you to wield upon this kingdom. I will go to war for you. I will kill all those who wish to harm you."

"Dax," she rasps.

"My men and I are yours if you wish it." My voice is softer than I ever expected it to be.

Her eyes widen when she realizes we are now encircled by my six brothers-in-arms. "What is that supposed to mean?"

With my other hand, I grip her thigh and explain, "I have watched you as often as you have watched them. I see the way you look at them with hunger and desire." My grip tightens until she looks back at me. "You are my Little Raven. I will only share you with them if you wish to have them. But only them. No one else."

I move my hand from her cheek to slide it through her hair, then tightly grip the strands. I force her face to mine as I growl in warning. "If I ever find out you were with a male other than us, you will see a true villain. Am I understood?"

She's panting as she looks into my eyes, and I watch her pupils shrink and then blow wide. "What would you do?"

I nip her lower lip, and she lets out hiss. I grin. "Test me, Little Raven, and find out."

Chapter Thirteen

Eira

Not going to lie… I hate walking the hallways of the castle by myself. Well, not every hallway. Mainly the ones with the covered mirrors. I could swear I heard whispers coming from them, which was even creepier because no one else seemed to notice them.

Why am I wandering the halls unguarded, you may ask? Kas. Kas is the reason. He has been acting weird ever since Dax's announcement claiming that I was theirs. It's his day to guard me, and I can't find him anywhere. Again. The last time I saw him was when we were all called to a meeting with Dax to discuss battle strategy. Which just so happened to be a few hours after his announcement.

Feeling eyes on me, I look around the room and find Kasim glaring. He honestly seems to be focusing all his energy on making sure I don't leave his sight. Huffing out a sigh, I ask, "What could I possibly have done now to earn your hostility?"

He shrugs, continuing to glare at me. "Nothing and everything."

I narrow my eyes. "Why are you glaring at me?"

"Is it rude to say I'm hoping you'll spontaneously combust?"

My eyes widen and I shriek, "Yes! Yes, it's very rude, Kasim."

He grins. "Then I'm hoping you'll spontaneously combust, Princess."

My gaze turns to Dax as I point at Kas. "Do something!"

Dax pinches the bridge of his nose as if he's frustrated with us both. "Kas, stop glaring at her! We all know you would rather be fucking her, so put up or shut up!" Dax takes a deep breath before continuing. "Now, can we get back to the reason I called this meeting, or should we all fuck Eira to get it out of our system so we can focus?"

They had not taken Dax up on his offer to fuck me, but I could tell there was heavy consideration for it. After hours of searching the castle, I finally found him in the combat zone. It's where all the recruits, and even soldiers, use to blow off steam by sparring. I march my way down the hill and yell once I'm closer to the circle of recruits he's buried in.

"Kasim!"

He turns to look at me, his eyes solid black. I've gotten used to their eyes changing; it doesn't make it any less off-putting, though. "What?" he grits out as rivulets of blood streak down his face.

It takes me a moment to reply because he doesn't have a shirt on, so I'm finally able to admire the skin he's kept hidden. His whole body is covered in ink. Swirls and images play across his chest and abdomen, and he has a handprint that matches the prince's. Intricate designs that I wish I had time to admire cover his arms. Shaking myself from the distraction, I put my hands on my hips and huff out, "You're supposed to be guarding me."

"Have one of the others do it. I'm busy," he sneers.

Rolling my eyes, I walk through the soldiers. They part easily, not wanting to be seen touching me, even by accident. When I'm right in front of him, I narrow my eyes. "Get your ass back to the castle now," I demand.

"Or what, Princess?"

Well shit... I didn't think that far ahead. "Or... I'll... step in front of every punch you're about to deliver to these men."

He arches a brow as if he doesn't believe me. I have no idea why I'm doing this. Why it's so important that I spend time with him. In all honesty, I miss our heated banter. I just want everything to go back to the way it was. He steps closer, eyes narrowed on me as he grunts. "Why would you do that? Why are you doing this?"

"Doing what?"

His eyes briefly flicker back to their normal hazel before shifting back to black again. "Treating me like someone you want to spend time with instead of the villain that I am."

"I-I don't understand. I don't treat you any differently."

"When we first met, you would have left me here to fight, not caring if I were guarding you or not."

My anger grows, and I can't stop myself from screaming, "I'm trying to have a serious conversation with you!"

"And I'm trying to subtly avoid it."

My fingers curl into fists as I huff out, "You are not being subtle at all."

He shrugs. "Don't care. Move."

Stomping my feet, I cross my arms across my chest. "No! I'm not leaving you here to fight. I'm having this conversation with you whether you like it or not. You're acting different too! Ever since Dax announced I was all of yours, you have been acting differently. You're constantly avoiding me!"

"That's not—"

I interrupt the lie he is trying to sell. "It is! You can't even look at me when we pass each other in the hall. You have refused to guard me completely!" I duck my head when the burn in my chest becomes too much. I'm not sure if it's anger from him avoiding me, or if I'm hurt because it feels like he resents me.

"Princess?"

I shake my head, and my vision blurs. My chest aches even more when I realize I'm hurt... it feels like he's rejecting me. At least when he used to spit his anger at me, I felt like I was seen, but now, I'm invisible. Not worth his time. "As much as I hate you, I miss you too. So can we *please* go back to the way things were? I don't care if you hate me, but please don't ignore me. Don't act as if I'm invisible." I take a shuddering breath before I whisper, "As if I'm nothing."

His finger tucks under my chin, and he lifts my face to meet his. A few stray tears manage to break through as I stare into his dark orbs. I watch his eyes shift, unsure where he's looking before they change into their natural dark hazel.

His eyes track the trail of my tears before meeting my gaze.

Eventually, he huffs out a sigh of defeat and nods. "Okay, princess."

"Really?" I ask with a hiccup.

His eyes flick away as he nods. With his jaw tight, he says, "Yeah. I'll pander to the spoiled princess."

Smiling, I wipe my face, wishing I could wipe away my moment of weakness. He looks back to me as he lets out a sigh and points toward the castle. "You shouldn't be out here. We could be attacked at any time, and you have absolutely no training."

Clasping my hands behind me, I ask, "Would you train me?"

"No," he replies without hesitation.

I look over my shoulder to find him looking at the ground. "Why not? If you trained me, I would be able to protect myself."

His eyes bounce up to me, shooting me a glare. "Because I have better things to do than train a spoiled princess." Biting my lip, I debate if I should really do what I'm about to do. Hum. He sees me smiling and asks, "What do you have planned, Princess?"

Unclasping my hands, I get ready to run. "Nothing!"

The moment I take off racing toward the house, I peek over my shoulder to see his eyes go wide.

"Princess!" he yells.

I laugh as I streak toward the castle, bumping into a few soldiers, and yell, "I'm sorry!" As I run, I can feel Kas's dark presence gaining on me.

When I feel his fingers graze my back, I squeal, but my legs keep moving as he slams into a wall. Ash sees me sprinting down the hallway, and his eyes go wide with alarm. "What's wrong?"

I laugh as I scamper past. "I'm running from a grumpy man!"

Ash turns to see who is chasing me and barks out a laugh. "I told you not to run!"

"Where's Dax?" I yell.

"In the great hall."

I manage to get all the way to the doors of the hall when I feel fingers graze my back again. With a screech, I push open the doors and then tumble inside as Kas grabs me. We roll across the floor before stopping at Dax's feet. Well, that's convenient.

I can't stop laughing as Kas stares down at me. "Caught you, Princess."

I look up to find Dax smiling at us. He chuckles and says, "You appear to have been caught, Little Raven."

I nod from my position on the floor. "I wanted to ask you a question."

"What question is that?"

"I was wondering if Kas could—" The rest of my words are mumbled when Kas covers my mouth with his hand.

"I told you no."

I smile sweetly under his hand, then bite one of the fingers covering my mouth. He hisses as he jerks his hand away, and I quickly finish speaking. "—train me how to fight!"

Kas glares down at me. "You are such a bad princess."

I grin widely as I look at him, then back to Dax. "So can he?"

He ponders the question for a moment before shrugging. "I don't see why not."

CHAPTER FOURTEEN

"**D**o the exercise we talked about, Kasim!" Dax yells, watching from the sidelines.

I didn't realize he had explained to Kas what to teach me. But it seems he is going off script and doing whatever he wants. If the gleam in his eyes tells me anything, it's that Kas is enjoying kicking my ass too much.

Wiping the sweat from my brow, I huff out, "Yeah, Kas. Do what your prince told you to do."

He shoots me a typical Kas glare from his position. "I have been improvising. An enemy won't care if you know how to perform a move or not. You should focus on protecting yourself instead of trying to get your sword to my throat."

"I'm trying!" I screech.

"You are possibly the worst person I have ever trained," he says with a smirk.

"He's trying to bait you, Snow Bunny," Ash shouts from the sidelines.

I know he is trying to bait me. That doesn't stop me from bristling at Ash's words. Seems Kas is back to normal after our talk the other day. I hate him. Well, I hate him right now. Groaning, I rub my shoulder. I *really* hate him right now. "Thanks for the encouragement. Are you naturally this much of a pain in the ass, or do you try extra hard just for me?"

He shrugs as he gets back into his fighting stance. "I may try a little harder just for you, Princess."

I hear Bene yell, "He's normally this much of an ass."

Kas's attention shifts to Bene, and he arches a brow. "Seriously?"

Taking advantage of the distraction, I rush him. But before I can lift my sword to his throat, he spins and has his sword's edge to mine instead. Ugh!

His lips brush against my ear as he chuckles darkly. "I'm a trained soldier. A minor distraction won't give you an advantage with me, Princess."

He removes the sword from my neck and backs up several steps. I'm convinced he's not holding back an ounce of his training. He enjoys watching me fail each time he holds his sword to my throat.

Huffing out an exhausted sigh, I scuff the grass with the edge of my boot. Branimir saddles up beside me while I continue to pout and kick the grass. Looking up, I find him smiling softly, and he says, "You are going to make it. This is only practice. The more practice you have, the better prepared you will be on the battlefield."

Taking another deep breath, I glare at his smiling face. "I think you are overestimating my skills here..."

He shrugs but continues to smile. "I'm not overestimating any-thing. If you can beat Kas once, then you'll be golden on the battle-field."

"He's enjoying my suffering immensely, Mir," I whine.

He chuckles as he rubs my sore shoulders. "I'm sure he is. But just think how elated you will feel when you finally beat him."

Looking around the circle, I see Alair giving me a thumbs up. Rev stands with his arms crossed over his chest but offers me a nod of encouragement. Dax is wearing a look of concentration as if trying to gauge the situation. When he notices me looking, he gives me a wink.

I hear a whooping sound and find Ash acting as my personal cheerleader. I suppose with that kind of encouragement, I don't have much choice but to quit my temper-tantrum.

With a final whimper, I move back into my fighting stance. My brain may say I need to continue this fight, but my body is groaning in protest with each movement.

Kas arches a brow. "You ready, Princess?"

I nod. "As ready as I'll ever be, Grumpy Man."

I roll over again as I try to find a comfortable position on my bed. No matter how I lie, I'm somehow on a bruise. They are worth the pain, though, since I was able to get my sword to Kas's throat one time. I was only able to do it once, but that doesn't matter. I feel accomplished, having managed that.

Twisting in my sheets again, I let out a frustrated sigh. I'm not going to be able to sleep anytime soon. Briefly looking around my room, I jump up from the bed and put on a robe and slippers. I could walk the castle, I guess? Avoiding the areas with the creepy mirrors of course. Guards are stationed everywhere, so I don't exactly need someone to follow me around. Dax had also made it *very* clear that if any of the guards touch me, they will lose their lives. So, castle investigation while avoiding the creepy hallways? That seems doable.

I open my door just enough to peek my head out. I don't see anyone, so I open it the rest of the way and step out into the hallway. Quietly closing the door behind me, I look to my left, then my right. Which way? Hum... I wonder if the kitchen has any leftover food. Oh! Maybe they have some leftover desserts! I do love their spiced butter apples. My mouth waters at the thought. But I would have to pass by a few mirrors to get to the kitchen. I don't give it much thought, just begin making my way there. I will just cover my ears and walk fast past the creepy mirrors.

On my way to the kitchen, I look for any open doors along the way. I may as well investigate while I can. It's on the way anyway. I nod to the guards as I pass, each giving me a nod in return.

As I peek into one of the open doors, I have to do a double take. The room is softly lit with candles, and standing next to the bed is Kas. But this isn't the Kas I normally see. His fingers are threaded in his hair, gripping it tightly, and swirls of darkness kiss his bare chest and weave around him through his cloth-covered legs.

When I quietly walk inside, I see that his eyes are squeezed shut, and his face is contorted in agony. I take a few steps closer and whisper, "Kas?"

His whole body jerks, and he growls, "Get out."

I know I should. I should run back to my room. But I can't. As much as I want to deny that I care about this man, my heart won't let me walk away when he's in this much pain. Taking a deep breath to steady myself, I step further into the room. I'll take a chance that he won't hurt me. I slowly make my way over to the edge of the bed and sit down.

A few wisps of darkness caress my skin, and I have to hold back a hiss from the sudden kiss of pure ice against my skin. Is this what he is consumed by right now? Complete and utter icy darkness? I shuffle a little closer so that I'm sitting right next to where he's standing.

"Get out," he grunts.

"No, I'm not leaving."

Time passes as silence surrounds us. After taking a deep breath, Kas settles on the bed beside me. I shiver when the shadows kiss my skin. Peeking out of the corner of my eye, I see his shoulders droop and his head slump forward.

I debate if I should try to comfort him or not. He isn't one to exchange niceties. Biting my lip, I decide to scoot a bit closer and lay my head on his shoulder. My body heat seeps out of me the moment of contact.

He stiffens, but he doesn't push me away. I feel my cheeks heat as I whisper, "I'm here. You can talk to me, or not, but I am here."

"Why are you here?" he rasps. He doesn't sound angry or irritated, which is odd for him. Instead, he sounds exhausted, like he's fought a thousand battles in his head during the last few minutes.

Taking a chance, I grab his hand to weave my fingers through his. I give it a squeeze as I say, "Because I care about you, you asshole. I may not like you. I may even hate you... occasionally. But that doesn't mean I don't care. Even if I don't really want to... sometimes."

His body slowly relaxes the longer we sit in silence, and eventually, the wisps of his dark power begin to recede as he takes deep breaths. "Why are you not in bed? You should be sleeping," he asks, his voice rough.

"I could ask the same of you."

He grunts before replying, "I... I don't sleep. Much."

"Why is that?" I ask quietly.

I watch as his thumb caresses the top of my hand, and he answers, "My mind is a scary place with the capability of being dark and demented."

"Is it not normal for villains to be plagued with dreams of that nature?" I try to joke, but it falls short as he stiffens. I squeeze his hand and quickly say, "Ignore me. That was meant to be a joke. So, you don't like your dreams?"

"No," he murmurs.

Damn, I've ruined this. He was finally opening up, and I made him feel worse. Caressing the back of his hand in return, I ask, "You are afraid of your dreams?"

"Yes," he rasps.

Trying to think of anything to help get his mind off his dreams, I remember his tattoos. I reach my free hand up to run my fingers around the inked designs on his forearm. "Do any of your tattoos have meaning?"

He's quiet for a moment before softly replying, "Not really. It was more of an escape."

"An escape?"

He huffs out a sigh. "My head can be a pretty dark place, Princess. Getting these tattoos caused physical pain, which helped with the psychological pain." He's silent another moment, but then his fingers tighten around my own. "But now that I'm saying it out loud, it sounds stupid."

I squeeze his hand back. "Not at all."

He hums in reply, so I hum back. We sit in comfortable silence for a while longer before determination starts to fill me, and I can't stay quiet anymore. My grumpy man is not acting like his typical grumpy self. So I'm going to fix it. Jumping up from the bed, I tug on his hand. "Come with me." He looks up at me, confused, and I can't help but smile when I see his eyes are back to their normal dark hazel instead of black.

He sighs. "Where are we going?"

I tug on his hand with a laugh. "Come on!"

His eyes narrow, but he relents and lets me drag him into the hall. Glancing over my shoulder, I find he's still glaring at me. I give him a wide smile, and he grunts.

"Stop that."

"Stop what?"

He gestures to my face with his free hand. "Doing that thing with your face when you're happy. It's making me nauseous." Then he grumbles under his breath, "This whole night is making me nauseous."

I laugh as I drag him toward the kitchen. I'm still determined to find dessert. But my heart feels lighter when I hear his annoyance; it's his version of normal. "I hate you, Grumpy Man!" I say but can't hide my giggle.

He huffs as he quietly says, "Hate you, too, Princess."

There's a flutter in my chest at his words. Because this time, they don't sound hateful. They weren't filled with his normal venom. The way he spoke almost felt... affectionate?

CHAPTER FIFTEEN

After my night with Kas, I need some time with my sunshine man. Is it weird I think of him as my ray of sunshine even though he's a villain? He's the oddest villain I'd ever met. He seems more the hero type rather than the villain, in my opinion.

I hear my nickname shouted behind me, making me jump. "Snow bunny!"

Peering over my shoulder, I find a blood-soaked Ash. My mouth gapes and I shout, "Why the fuck are you covered in blood!?"

He glances down at himself before looking back up to meet my gaze, a huge grin still in place. "Don't worry; it's not mine."

"I wasn't worried until you said that!" I grumble.

He glances back down at himself with a furrowed brow. "Although, I suppose some of it could be mine." He shrugs.

Pinching the bridge of my nose, I huff out, "There is so much there to unpack, but let's start with why you are covered in blood?"

He's chipper as he answers, "Torture, of course."

Arching a brow, I ask, "You or a prisoner?"

With a dramatic eye roll, he replies, "The prisoner, of course." Then he opens his arms out wide, flinging crimson blood on the pearl white walls. "Hug?"

I shake my head vehemently. "No. Don't you dare come close to me."

He arches a brow. "It's just blood."

"It's some random person's blood!" I screech.

"Maybe a bit of mine as well," he tries to reason as if that would change my mind.

I narrow my eyes. "My answer is still the same."

His gaze turns mischievous, and he asks, "Would you run?"

Confused by his question, I ask, "Why would I need to run?"

He lowers his arms and takes a step toward me. "Would you run?"

I point a finger at him, waggling it as I take a step back. "Don't you dare!"

Another step forward. "Oh, I dare, Little Snow Bunny."

With another step back, I say, "You will ruin my dress!"

He chuckles. "So... you're only worried about ruining your dress?"

Growling, I take another step back. "That's not what I meant. You just killed some random person! They could have been innocent."

"Is that what you are worried about? That I killed someone innocent?" He takes another step forward as he asks, "Would it ease your morals, if I said that the man I helped torture killed his entire family?"

I gasp as we continue this game of predator and prey. Alternating steps back and forward as we speak. "Why would he do that?"

He shrugs. "Why does anyone do anything in this kingdom?" He looks over my body before his eyes flash black for a moment. "I must say after a kill, my darkness is hard to control."

"What are you saying?"

He groans as he licks his lips. "I remember how delicious your tears tasted, Little Snow Bunny." He closes his eyes as if in ecstasy as he adds, "And your blood tasted even better."

"Asher," I whisper.

He moans, and his eyes turn black with the possibility of the chase. "Run, little bun-bun. Run as fast as you can. When I catch you, you'll cry tears of pleasure until my hunger is satiated." He takes another threatening step toward me. "Will you bleed for me too?"

Every alarm in my head is blaring. My instincts scream 'danger', so without hesitation, I turn and take off.

His laughter echoes through the hall. "Your fear is intoxicating."

I squeal as I turn the corner, heading in the direction of my room. If I can make it inside, I can lock the door. How fucked up is it that heat is pooling in my abdomen, and I can feel myself growing wet between my legs?

I've almost made it to my door when I feel strong arms encircle me. I scream as I'm lifted, twisted, and thrown into my room. It takes me a moment to gather my bearings, and I realize I'm in total darkness. The sound of the lock on the door clicking shut echoes in the quiet room.

I can't pinpoint Ash's location until I hear his deep voice behind me. "Looks like I've caught a bunny."

In a matter of seconds, I'm thrown onto the bed, and my dress is torn right up the center. My underwear is next to get ripped off, and Ash lets out a deep growl.

"Asher," I pant.

I scream when I'm suddenly filled with his cock. Tears prick at the corners of my eyes from the sudden fullness. He freezes for a moment before pulling out and slamming inside me again. His thumb is between us, and he begins massaging my clit.

The sudden burst of pleasure as he pumps into me again makes me cry out. "Come for me," he snarls.

I shake my head, thinking it impossible until he bites one of my nipples through the fabric. My core clamps down around him, and he growls, his face suddenly in front of mine. His tongue hungrily laps at the side of my face.

He's panting as he pounds into me and moans as he licks his lips. "Your fucking tears are addictive. My Little Snow Bunny cries so beautifully for me."

He pulls out of me suddenly, and I gasp at the sudden feeling of emptiness. He chuckles darkly as he moves down my body. Before I know it, his mouth is on my center, lapping at my release. He groans against me and pulls away. "How does Kas stay away from you when you taste this intoxicating?"

He continues to eat me as I slip my fingers into his hair, gripping tightly with each brush of his tongue. My thighs tighten around his head as the pleasure builds, and when he pinches my clit, it sends me headfirst into another climax.

My body feels like jelly when I relax my thighs, letting go of their death grip on Ash's head. He's grinning, and I look down to find the blood on the lower half of his face has been smeared away.

He hovers over me again, letting me feel his thick cock nudge my entrance. I whine, but he just chuckles darkly and lets his cock brush my sensitive cunt. "Is my bunny too tired to come again?"

I'm panting, but I shake my head no. He brushes his lips against mine before pulling away. I lick my lips, and I can taste myself. He hovers his mouth over my breast before biting down hard as he slams back inside of me.

I scream as I'm thrown into another orgasm, the stimulation and sensitivity too much. He growls and continues to thrust in and out of my tight channel. "Cry for me, bunny. Cry those delicious tears."

And I do. Tears stream down my face from overstimulation and pleasure, and he laps at the side of my face. I wait until he starts to pull away, then slip my hand around the back of his neck, pulling him close. I lift my head enough to brush my lips against his neck.

His rhythm stutters for a moment before his pace quickens once more. He grunts when I press my lips to his neck again, then open my mouth and bite down hard.

With a roar, he slams into me one last time before shuddering. I let go of his neck, and my head falls back onto the bed. I feel his cum fill me as he hovers over me, not moving. When he finally pulls away to meet my eyes, he's breathing heavily.

His black eyes are gone, instead, his pretty ocean eyes are looking back at me. He smiles softly as he gently pulls out of me. "Are you okay, Little Snow Bunny?"

My emotions are swirling so fast within me, I feel as if I'm in the center of a tornado. I don't even realize I'm crying until he coos, "Shh, it's okay. I'm here. Shh."

He rolls off the bed and gathers me in his arms, holding me close as he carries me into my bathroom. He sets me on the closed toilet seat before turning on the shower. Once the water is to his liking, he comes back over.

He gathers me in his arms and walks into the shower with me cuddled close. "I'm sorry," I hiccup.

"Shh, no need to apologize. I shouldn't have been that intense, forgive me. The darkness can be hard to control at times, especially after hours of torturing a person." He sighs and adds, "I usually find one of the guys to spar with until the darkness recedes."

"But I found you before you could find them, didn't I?"

Now that I've calmed some, he sets me down. "Yes," he says sadly. He begins washing my body with care, his brows pinched, as he ensures every inch of skin is taken care of.

"Ash," I whisper.

He hums, refusing to look me in the eyes. Not liking the turn in his mood, I place my hands on his cheeks, forcing him to meet my gaze. His eyes look haunted when they meet mine. "I didn't say no."

His eyes close on a sigh as my thumbs caress his cheeks. "I didn't give you much of a choice."

"Hey, look at me." His eyes slowly open to peer down at me, and I give him a smirk. "I didn't say no. Do you think for a moment that if I had said no, *REALLY* said no and meant it, you would have continued?"

His eyes shift away from me before he shakes his head. "No."

Pulling my hands from his face, I give his nose a boop. "Then give me a smile."

He rolls his eyes but smiles anyways. I grab for a washcloth, soaping it up. "Now, let's get all this blood off of you."

He groans, then shakes his head and chuckles. "I can't believe I fucked you with another man's blood on me."

I begin washing his body as I say, "Yeah... let's not do that again."

He arches a brow with a smirk. "What if it's my blood?"

I smack him with the washcloth. "Ash!"

He laughs and shrugs. "Just trying to feel out the boundaries."

Shaking my head, I sigh. "We will see."

Chapter Sixteen

I'm reading on my bed when I hear a knock on the door. Looking up from my book, I see Alair poke his head in. He's my guard for the day, but I didn't want to be a bother, so I decided to stay in my room. An odd thing, me worrying about being a bother. Arching a brow, I ask, "Yes, Alair?"

He looks around the room before stepping inside. "Why are you hiding out in here?"

I hold up my book. "I'm not hiding; I'm reading."

He gives me a cheeky grin before rushing across the room and jumping onto the bed beside me. I let out a squeal as I bounce. He jumps a few more times before finally landing on his butt.

I laugh and set my book down. "Is there a reason you've disturbed my reading time?"

He gives me pitiful puppy-dog eyes as he whines, "I'm bored, Eira!"

Shaking my head, I say, "I thought you all had training today. That's why I stayed in my room, so no one had to guard me."

He lets out a dramatic sigh. "I don't want to go to training. I want to have some fun!"

Knowing I'm about to get sucked into whatever scheme he has planned; I hop off the bed. Slipping on my house shoes, I turn to him with my hands resting on my hips. "Alright, Alair, what did you have in mind?"

His eyes widen with excitement. "Really?"

I nod. "You are my guard for the day, so you'll need an alibi for whatever ill-thought-out plan you have concocted."

He gasps as if offended. "It is a *very* well thought out plan, I'll have you know."

Arching a brow, I ask, "Who are you pranking?"

He gives me a skeptical glance. "I'm not sure if I want to tell you yet. You will try to talk me out of it."

I roll my eyes. "If I can talk you out of it, then you aren't confident enough in your plan to begin with."

He hums. "True."

"So who are we pranking?"

He looks around the room as if checking to see if anyone else is around. Then he crawls across the bed, so he's in front of me and replies, "Kasim."

I grin widely. "Oh yes. I'm totally in!"

He jumps off the bed, pumping his fist in the air. "Yes! I knew you would be my partner in crime."

I shrug and follow him out of the room. "I'm always down to mess with Kas."

He smirks. "I'll keep that in mind. You may regret saying that later."

I shrug. "A problem for another time."

He laughs, and we make our way down the hallway. We run into a few of the others as we head to Kas's room, but they think nothing of our mischief. Though, Rev gives us an arched brow as if he can feel our mischievous energy.

I shoot him a grin, and Alair mockingly salutes him before grabbing my hand. As we turn the corner, he whispers, "Are you ready for some fun, Little Fox?"

"Little Fox?"

He opens Kasim's bedroom door with a grin. "You are going to be my partner in crime, which means, you need a nickname. What's better than a cheeky fox?" He tugs on my hand, pulling me closer. His lips brush my ear, sending a shiver down my spine as he says, "My sly fox. Here to capture our hearts and minds."

I feel my cheeks flush as I whisper, "I find it hard to believe I've stolen your heart and mind."

He pulls away, snickering. "Then you haven't been paying close enough attention, Little Fox." He starts to search the room while dragging me along. "Now, what to do to cause optimal mischief?"

Glancing around the room, I can tell that Kasim clearly likes his stuff organized, almost obsessively so. "We could rearrange a bunch of his stuff?"

Alair tosses me a wide grin. "Yes!" he says excitedly as he turns back to the room and begins moving things around.

Shaking my head and laughing, I start to do the same. A few minutes pass, and I think I've done a pretty good job of rearranging his stuff when the sound of glass shattering behind me makes me freeze.

Turning around, I see Alair staring down at the floor with wide eyes. "What did you break?"

His eyes meet mine as I realize one of the few lights in Kas's room lies shattered on the floor. I have a feeling this practical joke is not going the way he planned. He points to the broken glass and asks, "Did you see that?"

Unsure if he's serious or not, I arch a brow. "Um..."

He shakes his head, then grabs my hand and drags me out of the room. "The correct answer is no; no, you did not. Now walk faster, Little Fox!"

Laughing, I try to keep up with his quick pace. "Why are we rushing?"

"Kas is due back from training any minute. We need to be far from here by then."

I can't stop giggling as he nods to each of the guards when we rush by. He looks over his shoulder, holding a finger to his lips. "Shh. Stop giggling! You are going to give us away."

I cover my mouth to dampen the sound, but I can't stop when I hear Kas yell, "Who the fuck was in my room?"

Alair gives up on his attempt at being sneaky and takes off running, dragging me behind him as we try to get away from Kas. "He's going to know it's us if you keep giggling!" he whisper-yells.

"S-Sorry," I say as I try to stop.

He looks over his shoulder and grins. "It's worth it to see that smile on your face, though."

My cheeks warm with his words. Seeing his smile and hearing him laugh makes it hard to believe that he is a villain. Are they really the villains? Or is that what I have been led to believe, I ponder. "Where are we going, Alair?"

My question is answered a moment later when he throws open the door to my room and pulls me inside. He slams the door behind him, leaning against it and trying to catch his breath. The air in the room grows thick when his eyes meet mine, and I see them shift to black.

"Alair?" I ask, breathless. I'm not sure if it's from running or the hunger I see in his eyes.

"I can see your nipples peeking through your dress, Little Fox," he says hungrily.

I look down to find that my nipples are indeed hard and easy to make out through my dress. I'm not sure where my boldness comes from, but when my eyes meet his, I smirk. "Our game was fun. Would you like to play another?"

He licks his lips as he pushes away from the door, stalking closer to me. "What do you have in mind?"

Dax had said they were all mine. That I belonged to all seven of them. Maybe I should start enjoying my time here and stop fighting what my body craves. That doesn't mean I'll give them my heart... just my body. I endured years of the king and his men using me for their pleasure; I think it's time I take some pleasure for myself. Taking a deep breath, I rip my dress over my head, leaving myself bare before Alair.

"Catch the fox," I taunt before taking off toward the bathroom.

There's a growl and, before I've even made it a few steps, his arms encircle me from behind. He nips my neck, and I can't suppress my moan. He slips a hand between my legs and hums against my neck. "Seems I've caught myself a fox. Now, what should I do with her?"

Slipping my hands up behind me, I tangle my fingers in his wavy, dark locks. I let out a needy moan when he slips a finger through my folds. He nips at my ear and growls, "What should I do with my fox?"

"Please her. Please your fox," I reply breathlessly.

His chest rumbles. "Now that sounds like a fun game. But let's make it even better." He flips me in his arms before pushing me up against the wall. He kneels on the ground in front of me, his black eyes looking up to meet mine. "How many times do you think I can make my fox come while screaming my name?"

"Alair," I pant.

He grabs one of my legs, lifting it and putting it over his shoulder, his breath tickling my hot center. "Let's see how long it takes for you to beg for my cock."

Chapter Seventeen

I'm slightly sore from my time with Alair last night, but there are certainly no regrets. With a groan, I pull myself out of bed to take a shower and get ready for the day. I try to think who my guard will be today as I shower.

After dressing in a simple gown, I make my way out of the room to search for Reverie. He's usually hiding somewhere around the castle; the issue is finding him. I had asked him once why he doesn't just guard me like everyone else.

"The shadows are where I belong," is what he had said. To be honest, I hate that he feels like the shadows are all he deserves.

Looking up and down the hall, I huff out a sigh, then turn to continue my search. I let out a squeal when Rev suddenly pops up in front of me, startling me. Holding a hand to my chest, I scold him. "I swear I will die of fright one of these days with you always jumping out of nowhere like that!"

He gives me a raised brow. "I did not jump, and it was not out of nowhere." He points to the dark room where he must have come from. "I walked out of that bedroom when you were turned the other direction."

Huffing out a sigh, I continue down the hallway. "It's like you are made out of shadows and darkness. I'm sure you would be horrible to play hide-and-seek with."

He hums beside me. "I have not played that game since I was a child."

With a grin, I turn to him. "Then we should play hide-and-seek!"

His brows furrow. "Why would we play a child's game?"

"It wouldn't be a child's game. You would be teaching me how to hide as well as you do. We could even make prizes for the winner."

His gaze turns thoughtful before he agrees with a nod. "I suppose learning how to hide and blend in could be helpful. What prize do you propose?"

Clapping, I reply, "If I win, then you have to spend one whole day out of hiding with me. That means you come to my door like a normal person and escort me around the castle without disappearing into the shadows."

His face sours at the thought, but he nods. "Very well. What is the prize if I win?"

Humming, I thoughtfully tap my finger to my lips. "If you win..." My eyes shift to his as I shrug. "I don't know. What do you want if you win?"

His chocolate eyes turn thoughtful before they are engulfed in black. There's a soft smirk on his face when he looks at me. "If I win that means I caught you, correct?"

Confused by the question, I nod hesitantly. "Yes."

He stands to his full height and says, "Alright, I catch you, I get you. That is my prize."

"Get me?"

He lifts a thumb to caress my lips, making me suck in a breath. "Did you think we couldn't hear your screams echoing through the castle?"

My cheeks flush. He bends till his breath brushes against my ear. "I want you to scream my name. So if I catch you, I get you." He pulls away, grinning wickedly. "Do you agree?"

I give a stiff nod.

"Words, Sunshine."

Taking a deep breath, I say, "Yes."

"Good," he growls.

I start to tremble, and I'm no longer sure if I want to win or lose. Though losing does sounds more appealing.

"Now... run and hide." He backs away from me and crosses his arms to wait.

With a look over my shoulder, I say, "I don't know where any of the good hiding places are."

He arches a brow with a smirk. "Then I suppose you better learn fast. You have one minute before I come searching for you. And your time starts, *now.*"

I let out a shriek and begin running down the hallway. I'm running so fast that I don't see the dark figure who steps out from around the corner until it's too late. I slam into a hard chest, squealing when I fall on my ass.

Groaning, I look up to find a wide-eyed Branimir. He holds out a hand and asks, "Are you okay? Why were you running so fast?"

Taking the offered hand, I let him pull me up. Looking behind me, I turn back. "I'm playing a game with Rev. Got to go! Bye!"

I go to pull away, but he doesn't release my hand. "What game are you playing?"

I tug on my hand, trying to get free. "Hide-and-seek. I only have so much time to hide. I've got to go, Mir!"

He smirks as he takes in my flustered state. "Are you trying to win or lose, Darling?"

I blush, and he chuckles as he releases my hand. He points down the hall. "If you want to lose, I recommend hiding in his room. But if you want to win, hide in Dax's."

I give him a nod and take off again. I hear him laugh behind me and call out, "Good luck."

As I run, I debate if I want to win or not. The game with Alair was very rewarding, and I imagine it would be the same with Rev. I did say I wanted to enjoy my time here. Making the decision to lose, I duck into Rev's room.

I attempt to calm my breathing as I look around. There aren't many places for me to hide in here. He keeps the bare minimum, which leaves either hiding behind the curtains or under the bed.

Rushing over to the bed, I shimmy under it as best I can. I've just managed to scoot all the way under when the door slams open. I cover my mouth to keep from yelping. The floorboards squeak with each step closer he takes; he's doing it on purpose. He knows how to move silently; he wouldn't be making a sound unless he wanted to. He knows I'm in here.

"Seems one of my brothers told you where to hide." There's another creak as he steps closer. "If I had to guess, it was Mir. He's the only one who would suggest my room as hiding place."

I look down when I hear the floor creak right next to my feet. Suddenly, he leans down, and Rev's eyes meet mine, a wide grin spreading across his face. "Found you."

With little warning, I'm ripped out from under the bed, and my wide eyes meet his pitch black ones as he straddles me. It feels as if he's looming over me with how much power radiates from him.

"Now to collect my prize, Sunshine."

I can't help but ask, "Why do you call me sunshine?"

His eyes briefly flash to their beautiful chocolate color before being consumed by darkness once more. "I find it hard to stay in the shadows when you are around. It's hard to hide when you shine so brightly."

My heart warms at his words, and I smile up at him. "Then, I will make sure to shine."

He hums before softly pressing his lips to mine and nipping at my bottom lip. He pulls away as I pant for more. "I have wondered what you taste like from the moment I watched Kas devour you."

My eyes flutter closed as I feel him shift down my body and lift the lower half of my dress up over my stomach. He spreads my legs wide and lifts my ass off the floor. I open my eyes to see my legs thrown over his shoulders and his dark eyes peering at me.

"You aren't wearing any underwear, Sunshine."

I shake my head in answer. I see the glint of his smile before the lower half of his face disappears. I suck in a breath when I feel his tongue lap up my center. I stretch my arms up behind me to grasp onto the lower rails of the bedpost.

Feeling him pull away, I whine and wiggle for more. He chuckles and says, "The taste of you will be forever seared into my mind now, Sunshine." He licks up my center once more before continuing, "Now, let's see if I can make you scream louder than Alair."

I do scream louder—multiple times—before his shadows engulf me. I know I should be fighting. Fighting against the darkness... against the sins these villains wish to infect me with. But at this moment... the darkness has never felt so good. Sin has never tasted so tempting.

"Are you ready for me?" he asks, growling, as he crawls up my body.

I'm delirious from all the orgasms he's given me, using only his mouth. Such a devilish mouth to go with such a sinfully beautiful demon of the shadows. "Yes," I pant breathlessly.

He pulls away to unbuckle his pants. My eyes shift to watch; I can't help myself from staring in raptured hunger as he pushes his pants down just under his butt, and I see the large bulge. He pulls his cock out of his underwear, and I can't stop myself from gasping.

Rev chuckles. "Enjoying the view, Sunshine?"

"Do you have metal in your cock?" I blurt out.

He hums as he lowers himself back down. The head of his cock brushes my wet entrance, and his lips are next to my ear as he replies, "I do."

His cool breath against my warm skin sends shivers down my spine. "Did it hurt?"

He chuckles again. "It was worth the pain. I'm sure you'll agree."

I'm confused by his answer until I feel the tip of his cock slip slowly inside of me, and I can feel the cool metal of one piercing near the base of the head of his cock. My fingers dig into the rail above me as I groan. "Oh my god..."

With the quick glimpse I had of his cock, I noticed there were piercings on the underside as well. I whimper as he continues his slow pace, each of the piercings sliding across my walls. Once he's finally seated completely inside, he slowly pulls out again.

The slow pace he sets has me panting. His piercings add an additional level of pleasure I never thought possible. My patience, however, doesn't last long as he continues his slow thrusts. "Faster!"

He hums against my neck, nipping, then sucking the area. "I do not wish to hurt you."

I can feel my orgasm just out of reach, and my frustration gets the best of me. "If you do not give me an orgasm right now, I will not allow you to fuck me with your pierced dick again!"

He slowly pulls out of me before slamming back into me. I groan as he bites my neck at the same time. "Again," I command. I hadn't asked for harder, but the way the metal on his cock hits all the right spots, makes me greedy for more.

His pace quickens, each thrust hard and fast as his breaths come faster. My fingers are starting to feel numb with how hard I'm gripping the rail above me.

The fire inside of me is growing, and I feel need tighten in my abdomen. Rev slides a thumb between my folds and begins circling my bundle of nerves.

"Come for me. I want my cock soaked. I want to be able to hear how fucking wet you are around me." He grunts as his free hand tightly grips my hip, and he continues to thrust in and out of me.

His words make me moan. My orgasm just out of reach.

"You will squirt around my cock," he demands, growling. "I want this floor drenched with your release. Come, now!"

He pinches my clit as he slams into me, and I scream when my body explodes. I do as I was told and soak his cock. I can vaguely hear the wet sound of it sliding out of me as he slams back into me with a roar of his own. The combination of our release slides down between my cheeks and pools between my thighs. I'm a little embarrassed by how much cum I produced with that orgasm. *Is that normal?*

I can feel Rev's quick breaths across my chest; his face is still buried in my neck. Slowly, he pulls away and looks down at me before sitting up. His cock is still buried inside me as he stares where we are joined with a groan. "So fucking wet."

My cheeks heat as he pulls out of me. He puts a hand under each of my thighs, lifting them up and out, so he can get a better look. He licks his lips, and I watch his eyes change from dark brown to pitch black. "You did so good, Sunshine. So good coming for me and doing what you're told," he praises in a deep voice. I watch as his cock begins to swell again. He lowers his face and licks between my swollen folds.

When his face comes back into view, his mouth and chin are soaked. He licks his lips as his dark eyes meet mine again. "I need more."

Before I can respond, my knees are over his shoulders again, and he puts his mouth back to work licking and sucking. Drinking in our combined release. My hands move from the rails and slide into his hair as I whimper with desire.

He's devouring me, and the only thing I wish is for him to never stop. Sin and salvation are different sides of the same coin... Right?

Chapter Eighteen

These men will be the death of me; I just know it. Why, you may ask? Because I am sore as fuck after being ravaged by not only Asher, but Alair and Reverie as well. The problem? All I can think about is how sexy Benedict looks leaning up against the bookshelf as he reads. Do these men release pheromones that I simply cannot resist? Or is my cunt that desperate to find release with these men?

I adjust on my chair as I try to figure out the best way to lay my book. It's positioned just right, so I can peek over it to watch Bene. His shirt is ruffled from training this morning, and his sleeves are rolled up to his elbows. I never thought forearms could be sexy, but his flex every time he flips a page.

He licks his finger to turn the pages, and the only thing I can think is how I wish he would lick me like that. Does that make me a sex fiend? I never found sex pleasurable until sex with these men.

I jump when I hear his silky voice. "Little bookworm, are you doing alright?"

Shaking myself, I give him a nod. "Yes. Yes, I'm fine. Why?"

He arches a brow as he points to the book in my hand. "You have been on the same page for the last twenty minutes." Then he gestures to the other books around me. "Although, I suppose I should recant my nickname of bookworm with the hoard of books around you."

I smirk as I look around at the hundreds of books surrounding me. "What would you call me instead?"

Closing what he was reading, he crosses his arms, still leaning against the bookshelf. He gives me a thoughtful look before nodding. "You would be a book dragon. A dragoness, I suppose."

Humming, I smile. "A dragoness. That does sound better than bookworm."

He points to the book still in my hand. "Now, what was running through that mind of yours that kept you on the same page for twenty minutes?"

My cheeks heat, and I hide behind the cover of the book. "I couldn't concentrate on the words. And it was not twenty minutes," I mumble.

He chuckles as I hear his footsteps near. "We have been in the library for thirty minutes, and I have been watching you the whole time. It was twenty minutes of you not flipping a single page."

I wiggle in my seat as embarrassment fills me. "Like I said," I whisper, "I couldn't concentrate."

Bene runs a finger over the top of the book and pushes it down, away from my face. His brown eyes, framed with wisps of platinum-blonde hair, fill my view. "Now, what could possibly pull your concentration away from such a captivating book, Dragoness?"

I bite my lip before whispering, "I was distracted by the only thing able to pull the attention of a dragoness away from her hoard."

He smiles as he kneels in front of me. "And what could do that?"

"A dragon," I murmur.

He slips his hands under my dress and caresses my legs, sliding them up to my thighs. I suck in a breath as he grins. "I imagine not just any dragon could pull you from your hoard." His thumbs caress the inside of my thighs as he asks, "What's so special about this dragon?"

Finding it hard to concentrate with the sudden rush of pleasure, I stutter, "He-he's handsome."

He hums thoughtfully as he drags my underwear down my legs. "There are many handsome dragons, Eira. What's special about *this* one?"

Warmth pools in my stomach as I watch his eyes shift to black before returning to their normal cinnamon color. "His eyes," I say breathily.

Bene smiles as he lifts my dress up to my hips. "What about his eyes?"

"They are warm and comforting like cinnamon."

Humming, he slips his hands under my ass, pulling my hips toward him, and I let out a squeak. "What else has caught your attention?" he asks.

He massages my ass before moving to my thighs, drawing small circles against my skin. Clearing my throat, I reply, "Um... he loves books."

He nods as he lowers his face to my center. "Hum... maybe you should read that page you've been stuck on for twenty minutes."

Not arguing, I open the book to the page I was stuck on and begin to read. I screech when he pinches my clit. "Out loud, Dragoness."

Nodding, I begin reading. "There once was—" I hiss when his hot mouth sucks on my clit.

He chuckles and pulls away. "Keep reading."

I whimper but attempt to continue. The moment I begin talking he continues his torture. "There once was a ruler who wished to conquer all of the lands... fuck."

His tongue slips from my center, taking one more long lick before pulling away. "I don't think that's how it went. Maybe I should stop, so you can read properly."

Shaking my head, I clamp my thighs around his head and send him a glare. "Don't you dare."

"Then keep reading."

There is no way I will be able to read while his tongue is inside me. I'll just have to improvise. "There once was a ruler who wished to conquer all of the lands," I say, growling.

He smirks as he lowers himself, and I squeeze my legs, so he won't be able to pull away again. Throwing the book to the side, I slip my fingers into his long hair. "But he found a female more enticing."

He hums against my core as I rub myself against his face, needing more. My fingers tighten in his hair as I pant out, "He... he found her... hypnotizing."

Bene growls when I use his hair to tug him closer. I look down to find his endless, black pits staring back up at me. Grinding myself against him, I groan. "He loved to pleasure her."

His tongue laps at me as he slips a finger inside. He strokes slowly and sucks on my clit, causing my back to bow. The finger stops, and I whine but continue. "Fuck... fucking her with his tongue... until she came. The end."

He slips another finger inside me, curving them to hit just the right spot that makes me pant for more. "Yes... yes, just like that."

His strokes become faster as I tug on his hair, feeling the pleasure building. "Fuck her! Fuck her! Fuck her!" I scream.

He growls, managing to break the hold my legs have on his head. He pulls away, falling backward, taking me with him. I didn't have enough time to realize what was happening before he slams his cock inside.

My hands grip his chest as he grips my hips with each thrust. His eyes are dark pits as he groans and asks, "Do you enjoy your dragon's cock?"

"Yes."

He grunts with a hard thrust. "So needy for my cock."

"Yes," I cry.

His fingers dig into my hips, and I just know they'll leave bruises as his pace increases, hitting that perfect spot each time. "Cream for me. So wet and tight," he snarls.

I scream, and he slams into me as stars fill my vision. Letting out a low, rough grunt, he continues to thrust in and out of my tight channel. He slips his thumb between us and massages my clit, making me whine as the pleasure renews.

My nails dig into his chest as he continues to fuck me. "Come!" he barks.

I shake my head. I can't possibly, even though I can feel the pleasure building again. I feel him slip a hand from my hip, up my body, and into my hair. He fists my long locks, pulling me forward. My wide eyes meet his black orbs as he demands, "I told you to *COME*, Little Dragoness."

The pleasure-pain is too much when he bites my shoulder at the same time as he pinches my clit. He slams into me again just as I come with a scream.

He growls, and I feel his release. We catch our breaths while he holds me in his arms. I can hear his rapid heart beat as I lie there. I whine when his cock slips out as he lifts me higher up onto his chest.

"Shh. We won't be moving for a while."

I nod as Bene runs his fingers through my hair, massaging my scalp. I groan and melt into his body, closing my eyes as I relax.

"Rest, my Dragoness. I'll guard you and your hoard."

CHAPTER NINETEEN

Today it is Mir's turn to guard me, and I'm hiding out in my room. Is it cowardly to hide from a man in my room? Yes. Do I regret hiding from him? Maybe. But the poor man blushes the whole time he is around me. Do I make the man that uncomfortable? He is very sweet, and the last thing I want to do is make him miserable the entire time he's standing guard. It makes me wonder why he is still on the guard rotation if I make him that uneasy.

Sighing, I throw a pillow over my face. Asher is always happy to see me, and Kas is... well... Kas. He doesn't seem bothered by my presence. Rev has been staying out of the shadows more when around me. And Alair drags me along to play jokes on anyone and everyone. And Bene... Bene will sit with me for hours, reading.

Maybe I just don't click with Mir? The thought makes my chest hurt. I scream into the pillow, then scream again when I hear, "Is screaming into your pillow normal for you?"

Ripping the pillow from my face, I see Mir standing at the end of my bed with an arched brow. The moment his eyes meet mine, pink skates across his cheeks. Red hair falls in front of his eyes as he tilts his head with a smirk.

Covering my face with a pillow again, I mumble, "I make you uncomfortable."

"I couldn't hear that. What did you say?"

"I make you uncomfortable," I yell into the pillow.

Mir yanks the pillow away from my face as he sits down beside me. He throws it aside before looking back at me. His ears are pink now as well. "Now, repeat that."

Sighing, I look to the ceiling. "I said, I make you uneasy."

"What gives you that idea?"

Without looking at him, I gesture in the direction of his face. "You're always blushing and quiet when I see you. You only do that when I'm around."

He's quiet for a moment before I feel a finger on my chin. He turns my face till our eyes meet. "Is that why you have been hiding in your room all day?"

"Yes," I whisper.

He hums, and his smirk drops. "I promise that is not the reason I am like this around you."

Rolling my eyes, I try to fight his grasp on my chin. "What other reason could you have for acting this way?"

I gasp when his grip on my chin tightens, and his eyes flash black. "Did you ever think that maybe my thoughts of you aren't as innocent as you believe? That thoughts of desire cause this blush to creep across my face?"

"Branimir?"

He groans. "Fuck, I love the way my name sounds on your lips. It makes me wonder how that beautiful mouth will feel wrapped around my cock."

I can't help myself. I whisper his name again. "Branimir."

He groans and releases his grip on my face, only to crawl toward me and hover above me. "My cheeks stain red because my thoughts about you are not sweet and innocent."

"Oh? Then what are they?"

"Dark and lustful, Darling," he purrs.

"Show me," I pant.

He grins. "So eager to hear my dark thoughts?" he teases, then lowers his face to my neck, and I hear him sniff. He growls and drags his tongue up my neck. "Did you know you smell like apple blossom?"

"No." I squeak as he nips at my neck.

"Apples are my favorite treat. Maybe I should eat you for dessert?"

"Yes," I whine.

He groans as he pulls away. My eyes widen when I see his are consumed by darkness, and swirls of black mist kiss my skin. "I'm very hungry, Darling." Before I can say anything, he rips my dress down the middle.

"Mir!" I squeal. "Not another dress!"

"We will buy you more. Now let me admire my dessert." He pins my arms above my head with a grin and orders, "Keep those there for me."

As his eyes roam over my body, I begin to feel self-conscious. I start to lower my arms back down, but then swirls of darkness solidify around my wrists. He tsks, "Ah, ah, ah, Darling." His eyes flare as he commands, "Stay."

I gasp when I feel the cold kiss of darkness grip my wrists. "You can control the darkness?"

He licks his lips as his eyes continue to rove over every inch of me. "I can do many things with my darkness." He slides his hands up my thighs as he hums. "Would you like a demonstration, Eira?"

My breath hitches as cold whispers across my underwear before Mir slips them down my legs. Dark fingers trail over my body and pinch my nipples. "Mir," I whine.

Invisible straps tighten around my ankles, spreading me wide for him. "So beautiful. Say my name again."

I drop my gaze to find him completely naked, his cock on full display. I can't help but lick my lips as I see that his penis is pierced as well, but in completely different spots. "You have metal just like Rev."

He hums and smirks. "I do, but I can tell you that my cock will feel completely different than his."

Of this I have no doubt. Four metal balls sit around the head of his cock compared to the single one Rev has under the head of his. Mir starts to stroke himself and, licking his lips, he says, "I've got a hidden piercing, too, but you only get to play with that one if you're a good girl." He positions himself at my opening, swirling the head around my entrance before entering me in one quick thrust.

"Branimir!" I scream. I feel so full, and his piercings stroke a completely different level of pleasure than Rev's.

He groans, and his darkness erupts around us. "So *fucking* tight." He pulls out before slamming back in to the hilt. I shriek as the metal of his piercings stroke my slick walls, making my body sing with pleasure.

Tendrils slip between us, and I hiss when I feel cold fingers caress my clit. The vast difference between warm and cold increases my pleasure. The darkness around my wrists tightens as he begins to pant. "I want to mark you, like Dax. Make you mine! I want to make you scream like Rev." He growls. "He told me how soaked you were for him."

I keen as I try to arch closer to him. "Mir..."

His voice is deep as he continues, "How the floor was covered in your release. How he drank from you for hours."

He lowers his mouth to my neck and bites down. Hard. Releasing his hold, he then licks away the sting. Moving to the other side, he bites down again, repeating the action over and over until my upper body is covered in teeth marks.

He looks down to admire his work as he pumps inside me. His eyes flare, and he grins wildly. "*Mine*," he growls. "You are going to come for me like a good girl."

He lowers again, covering my breast with his mouth. He sucks hard before biting down while dark tendrils of ice pulse around my clit. "I'm a greedy bastard. I want you dripping. Come!" he demands.

I scream and clamp down on him, arching with pleasure. But the pleasure doesn't ebb as he continues to thrust into me. My tight channel is strangling his cock.

He groans and praises, "So good, Darling."

The cold tendrils of his darkness swirl around my fingers, and I stroke the solid shadows holding my palms. Mir's hips stutter as his eyes flick up to mine. I can't stop the grin that creases my face as I stroke his darkness again, and he groans. His eyes flutter closed as his head drops back.

His thrusts grow erratic as I continue to stroke the darkness. His breathing is labored as he slams into me one final time, roaring his release. I can't stop my own orgasm as the world explodes around me. The pleasure of knowing I brought him to climax by stroking the darkness he commands. He pants above me as the darkness recedes, and the hold on my wrists and ankles disappear.

His lips brush against mine as he asks softly, "Are you well, Darling?"

I can't muster a reply, so I hum my confirmation. His eyes shift to their brilliant forest green, and his deep red hair sticks to his sweaty face. He gives me a soft kiss before pulling away.

I whine and he chuckles. "I'll be right back, Love."

My chest feels fluttery at the endearment. The bed shifts as he slips off, but it's only a few moments later that I feel a warm, damp cloth against my sensitive folds. I whimper as he gently cleans me up, then I hear a splat.

"What was that?" I mumble.

"I threw the cloth on the floor. I'll pick it up later." He slides back into bed, pulling me into his arms. Pressing a kiss to my forehead, we settle together in the softly lit room.

"I should get up and…" My mind blanks as I try to come up with a reason to leave the bed.

"And what, Darling?"

"I have no idea," I say and sigh. "You're too comfortable for me to think clearly."

He chuckles as he pulls me closer. "Then let's just lie here for a while."

"I suppose I don't have anything better to do."

"Exactly."

"A few moments pass before I get the courage to say, "You don't have to be afraid to show me what you want or who you are. I don't mind your dark and lustful thoughts."

He chuckles. "I will remember that from now on, Darling."

Humming in reply, I snuggle deeper into him. A random question pops into my head, and I can't stop myself from blurting it out. "Does anyone else have fancy dicks?"

Mir snorts. "Only Rev and I have the so-called 'fancy dicks'."

I shrug. "That's too bad. I like them."

The sound of his laughter surrounds me, and the darkness closes in around me. I fall asleep with a smile on my face.

Chapter Twenty

Trudging around my room, I debate if I should find Dax. He will be able to answer my questions about the book; it was in his library after all. But I don't want to disturb him. I know the guys are in a war meeting and then they have training. It is why I will be staying in my room; that way no one needs to guard me, and they can train.

Groaning, I pull the book away from my chest and peer down at it. I want to ask why an apple is on the cover of a *Spells and Curses* book. It is an odd choice for a cover. My curiosity is getting the best of me.

Huffing out a sigh, I let my curiosity win. Marching to the door, I swing it open, only to find Branimir with his hand poised to knock. His wide eyes meet mine, and he lowers his hand. "Oh, um... I just wanted to tell you we are on our way out to train."

Smiling, I nod. "Have fun."

He smirks and leans forward, brushing his lips against mine briefly before stepping away with his usual bright pink cheeks. "I don't believe training is supposed to be fun, Darling."

Rolling my eyes, I amend, "Then have a horrible time."

He chuckles and gives me a nod. "Will do." He makes his way down the hall as Bene takes his place.

Pointing to the book in my hand, he smiles. "Don't bury your nose into too many books without me, little bookworm."

I'm a bit surprised to find the rest of the males patiently waiting while Bene and I talk. Are they all waiting to greet me before training? Nodding distractedly, I say, "I won't."

He presses a kiss to my forehead before pulling away and following Mir. Shaking my head with a smile on my face, I find Alair moving closer to take his place. "Do I get greeted by each of you before you leave?"

He shrugs and boops me on the nose. "Stay out of trouble. Unless you plan to invite me, Little Fox."

Laughing, I say, "I'll make sure to keep my ideas a secret till you return."

His grin is wide as he starts to walk backward after the others. "Sounds like a plan."

"Look where you're going!" I call, but he just gives me a wink and turns around.

Asher gives me a big smooch on the cheek before following Alair. "Have fun today, Snow Bunny!"

"Be safe," I yell back.

With a mock salute, he turns, running after Alair. I turn to find Rev standing in front of me in all his dark glory. Arching a brow, I ask, "Decided not to pop out of the shadows in greeting today?"

The corners of his lips twitch as he lifts a hand to caress my cheek. "Not today, Sunshine."

I turn to press a kiss to his palm. "Then, I look forward to the rest of the day."

He hums, pulling away. "Cheeky, Sunshine."

I hold my free hand up and wiggle my fingers. "Spooky, Shadow."

He grunts, and I swear it's a laugh. I've never heard him laugh, so I'm counting it as a win. With one last shake of his head, I see the tilt of his lips as he heads in the direction of the others.

I point to Rev as I turn to Kas. "I made him laugh!"

Kas is wearing his typical scowl as he arches a brow. "Is that what you call a laugh?"

With narrowed eyes, I say, "Yes! When it comes to you and Rev, it's hard to even get a smile. I'm counting it as a laugh."

He takes a step forward, crossing his arms. "Where are you headed?"

"If you must know—"

He interrupts, "I must."

I can't help but roll my eyes. "As I was saying, if you must know, I am going to talk to Dax."

He snaps his fingers over his shoulder and orders, "Take her to see the prince."

My eyes widen when two soldiers step away from their posts to stand behind Kas. "I can go by myself."

"Do you know which way to go, Princess?" he asks, unable to hide his smirk.

Huffing out a sigh, I growl, "No."

He gives a satisfied nod. "Off you go."

"I hate you," I reply as I pass him.

He snorts and turns to make his way down the hallway. "Hate you, too, Princess."

I follow quietly behind the guards as they guide me to Dax. It's only a few moments before we are standing in front of wooden double doors. The guards give me a bow, then return to their posts.

I knock and wait a moment before opening the door. "Dax, I was wondering—" I immediately slam the door closed with a squeal.

Dax laughs on the other side. "Come in, Little Raven. I'm done playing."

"I think I'll stay right here," I reply with an edge of hysteria. I knew these men were dark. I've seen Ash covered in blood. On the other hand, though, I was not ready to see a man hog tied with an apple stuffed in his mouth and covered in blood.

"Come in, Eira. I feel this is a great learning moment for you."

"I'd rather not," I whisper.

I hear footsteps, and the door suddenly swings open. I jump back with a squeak. He holds out a hand with a dark, deceptive smile. "Come now, Little Raven. There's nothing to fear."

Right, nothing to fear, except for the men I keep forgetting are the villains. Taking a deep breath, I slip my hand into his, and he escorts me into the room. My eyes automatically drift to the bloody male. I jump when I hear Dax's deep voice explain, "This is his punishment for attempting to spy on me for my father." He shrugs as we pass the man, stepping up onto the platform where the throne sits.

He escorts me over, gesturing for me to take a seat. Doing as I'm told, I hold the book closer to my chest. He smiles as he steps away, briefly looking back down at the man. "What brought you to me, Little Raven?"

"Right." My voice comes out high-pitched. Clearing my throat, I try again. "Right, um... I had a few questions about this book I found in the library."

He hums as he circles the restrained man. "What questions do you have?"

Holding the book out so he can see it, I say, "First, I'm wondering why there's an apple on the cover of a *Spells and Curses* book."

Humming thoughtfully, he pulls the apple out of the man's mouth. The man begins to yell for help but is cut off when a tendril of darkness covers his mouth like a gag. Dax doesn't seem bothered by the man as he inspects the apple in his hand. "Do you know the symbolism behind an apple?"

I shake my head, and he continues, "Knowledge, immortality, and temptation." He points to the book in my hand. "That book holds all three."

Arching a brow, I ask, "What do you mean?"

His eyes flick from the apple to me. "Did you know my father used apples to gain his power?"

My eyes widen in shock as I reply, "No."

Holding the fruit up, he frowns. "He would poison them. Infect them with a curse." I watch as the bright red apple in his hand turns to a sickening brown. "The only issue with that is you cannot just hand an apple like this to anyone and expect them to eat it."

I watch with wide eyes as the darkness around the man's mouth disappears, and Dax shoves the rotten apple back into his mouth. He looks back at me with dark eyes as he wipes his hand on his shirt. "You have to bake it into something. That is why the cooks know so many apple recipes. It's also the reason apples are the only fruit that will grow in this god-forsaken wasteland."

I point at the man as Dax continues walking my way. "Did... did you just poison him?"

He shrugs. "He deserves a slow death." Clapping his hands, he sits on the arm of the throne. Tapping the book in my hands, he says, "That book contains forbidden knowledge and words of immortality. It contains things that any power-hungry being would be tempted by."

"Why is it in your library?" I whisper.

His eyes turn pitch black as he growls. "It belonged to my father."

That makes a lot of sense. Opening the book to the page I bookmarked, I hold it out to Dax. "I was wondering what this passage meant."

He leans in, looking at the page, and gives me a sad smile. "It's a spell, Little Raven."

"But what does it mean?"

His eyes shift back to bright blue, but they seem to have lost a bit of their shine, and he sighs. "It is how the others share my curse. How they share the darkness with me, so that I do not bear it alone."

My brows pinch as I close the book. I cover his hand with my own, giving it a squeeze. "What does the spell do?"

He looks away as he answers, "It binds your soul with another. Forever bound."

My eyes widen. "I thought magic was gone; it was outlawed years ago."

He looks down at my hand still holding his. "It was outlawed after my father became consumed with the dark magic that book gifted him." Then he adds in a whisper as if not meant for my ears, "as well as the mirror he found."

"Mirror? Is that why you have all the mirrors covered in the castle?"

He gives me a false smile that doesn't meet his eyes. "A story for another day, Little Raven. Anyway, as I was saying, just because magic was outlawed does not mean that magic is gone. Dark magic does not just disappear because it is outlawed."

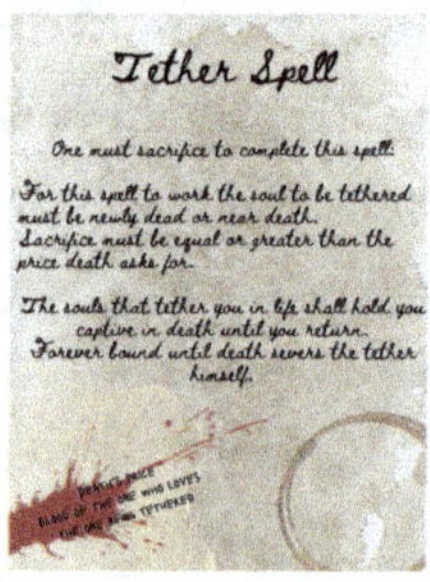

CHAPTER TWENTY-ONE

I can't see shit, and I'm getting irritated. The guys are working on a plan to infiltrate Arcelia. They want to see how close they can get and possibly assassinate the king. If they succeed, Dax will become king. Even though I am the rightful heir to the Arcelia throne, the thought of him being in charge doesn't bother me as much as it did before.

"I can't see anything! You guys are planning an invasion, and I can't see a single thing. Why is this damn table so tall!?"

Dax snorts as he turns to Branimir. "Can you get something for her?"

Branimir looks between Dax and me. "What do you propose I do? I can look around the castle for a stool, or would you rather me mount her on something?"

Raising a brow, I smirk at Branimir and ask, "Like a pike or a sex swing? I would take either, at this point, to see the table." I watch as his eyes snap up to meet mine.

His cheeks are as bright as his red hair, and his freckles pop against his now-crimson cheeks. His mouth gapes open for a moment before he stutters, "That's... that's not... I didn't mean it like that!"

Tears stream down my face as I laugh. The poor man easily gets flustered, and his blush only fuels my laughter. Now that I know he loves dark and dirty sex makes it even better. The other men around us laugh as Branimir walks off.

I hear him grumble as leaves the room, "I'll mount you on the damn wall if you keep laughing at me like that."

After a few more moments of laughter, I finally settle. Standing up on the tips of my toes, I try to see over the table. I hear a few snickers from the guys as Branimir stomps back into the room and walks up next to me.

I turn to watch him hammer something into the wall right behind the war table. With a huff, he turns back around, now facing me. "There, I found something to help you see," he grumbles.

My head tilts as I try to figure out what it is he just mounted. "What is it?"

Rev snickers as he answers, "It's a weapons' rack."

I arch a brow in his direction. "A weapons' rack?"

"Yes, Princess. A weapons' rack," Kas says.

"Can I punch him?" I ask the room.

Kas grins wildly as Dax shakes his head, looking amused. "No, you cannot punch Kas."

My eyes narrow on Kas's smiling face. "Are you *sure* I can't punch him in the face?"

Dax laughs as he looks between the two of us. "Yes, I'm sure, Little Raven."

I look at Dax with a frown. "What if I just break his nose?" I hold up my hand with my index finger and thumb a smidge apart. "Just a little?"

He shakes his head, still smiling. "You cannot wound one of my warriors before a major battle. Maybe next time, Little Raven."

Huffing out a dramatic sigh, I grumble, "Fine." Turning my attention back to the weapons' rack, I ask, "So how is this going to help me?"

Ash walks over to me with a smile, his eyes full of mirth. He takes my hand as he ushers me over to the new addition on the wall. He slips his hands to my waist, and before I can protest, he lifts me in the air and sets me up on top of the rack. He gives me another smile. "There. Now you can see everything."

He releases his hold, and I immediately latch onto the sides of the rack. "I'm not sure how safe this is."

Dax waves a dismissive hand in the air. "If it can hold our weapons, it can certainly hold you, Little Raven."

"That isn't the point, Dax!"

His eyes meet mine as he arches a brow. "What is the point then, Little Raven?"

"I'm... I'm not really sure what my point was. But I did have one!"

Humming, he turns back to the table. "Well, once you remember be sure to inform me."

"I will," I say haughtily.

Dax chuckles and begins moving pieces around the table as well as marking a few areas on a map. I point to one of the red X's and ask, "What is that?"

All seven men turn to see what I'm pointing to. Extending my arm, I shake my finger at the X, my other arm still wrapped tightly around one of the poles extending from the rack I'm perched on. "That. What is that?"

Bene looks back to the table, hovering over what he thinks I'm pointing to. "This?"

Shaking my head, I respond, "No, the one right next to it." He shifts his finger over to the red X I'm asking about, and I grin. "Yes, that one."

His eyes meet mine. "This indicates a hostile area that we should avoid letting our forces enter; it's a death zone. Too many of the king's undead in that area."

"Oh." I notice several more red X's marking the map along with a few green. "What does the green mean?"

Alair is the one who answers this time. "Green indicates the safest spots. There should be minimal undead there, and our best chance to infiltrate the castle is from those points."

"So where will I be?"

Kas snorts out a laugh. "Where will you be? You will be here where it's safe, Princess."

My eyes immediately narrow on Dax. "I will not be left behind like some damsel. I'm just as much a part of this as you are."

Asher sighs dramatically. "We aren't saying you aren't part of the kingdom, Snow Bunny. We want only to keep you safe."

Rev tries to reason with me. "You aren't trained for battle, Sunshine. It won't be safe for you on the battlefield."

My eyes never waver from Dax's as I matter-of-factly state, "I *will* be on that battlefield. One way or another."

"Little Raven," he warns.

My eyes narrow on him. "He killed my family."

"Maybe there's a way we could convince her otherwise," Mir suggests with a smirk.

My eyes snap to Mir, and I say tersely, "You will *not* convince me otherwise."

His eyes flare black as his grin widens. "Is that a challenge, Darling?"

"No. That is not a challenge. It is a fact. I *will* be on that battlefield."

He begins slowly walking toward me. "I believe that is a challenge."

Bene chuckles as he follows Mir. "Let's see how she feels after a few orgasms."

I point to them when they come closer. "You are not buying my cooperation with orgasms."

Alair smirks but stays by the war table. "I'm sure we can find a way to change your mind."

I grip the rack I'm sitting on as Mir tries to pull me down. "No! You are not going to change my mind by fucking me!"

Rev hums and says, "So you're saying there's a chance we can change your mind."

"No!" I squeal as Mir pulls me off the rack and throws me over his shoulder.

Smack. Did he just smack my ass?

"Be good, Darling."

I will *never* admit how wet I got from that slap. "You can't just *FUCK* me to get what you want!" I scream as I try to wriggle out of Mir's strong grasp.

"I think you highly underestimate our ability to fuck that attitude out of you," Kas says with a dark grin.

I hear a crash and look over to find Dax clearing the war table. Figures and battle strategies go flying when Mir slams me onto the table. I glare at each of them as they hold me down. "I think you overestimate your ability to fuck me well enough to make me change my mind."

Bene laughs and looks at Dax. "I believe that was a challenge, Your Highness."

The guys take up positions around the table just like they did when the king visited. Each of them holds down a wrist or an ankle, and dark swirls of shadows fill the room as their eyes turn to black pits. I gasp when Dax climbs onto the table, slowly crawling until he is hovering right above me. "Let's see if we can change that mind of yours, Little Raven."

"Never."

He grins down at me as if to say 'challenge accepted', then he pulls his pants down enough to release his cock. My eyes widen as he groans and pumps it a few times. Pre-cum drips from the tip and he growls "I'm sure after taking seven cocks, your mind will be too hazy with lust to argue."

Chapter Twenty-Two

D ax slams into me, making me scream, and he snarls as power pulses around us. "So fucking tight," he groans.

My fingers curl into fists as I moan. My eyes snap to Mir when I feel cold tendrils slip between Dax and me. He licks his lips, his voice hoarse. "I bet you're already soaked for our prince."

Bene pinches my nipple, and I scream as I tighten around Dax. He growls, wildly pumping into me, chasing his orgasm. "Fuck... she's soaking my cock."

I'm in the midst of pleasure when Dax snarls with his release. I'm panting, trying to catch my breath, when he looks down at me with a smirk. "Have you changed your mind yet, Little Raven?"

I shake my head as I huff, "No."

He smiles. "Good." Turning to Asher, he barks, "Fuck your Snow Bunny well, brother."

I groan as Dax pulls out. Power pulses around the room again, and Asher takes his place without hesitation. He slowly slides in to torture my sensitive cunt, smirking when I whine for more.

He caresses my bottom lip with his thumb and continues his slow pace. "Your mouth looks so fuckable." He pushes his finger between my lips and groans. "Suck me like you would my cock."

I wrap my tongue around his finger and suck. Hard. His hips stutter and I grin. Then, I suck his finger just as slowly as he's fucking me. His eyes narrow when he catches onto my game. He grips my chin with his other hand while his thumb is still in my mouth. *"Suck me,"* he commands.

I release suction on his thumb and try to speak through his tight grip. *"FUCK ME."*

His fingers next to my head curl into a fist as he pushes his thumb deeper into my mouth. My eyes water, and I'm forced to hold back a gag. He offers me a dark smile when my eyes water and demands with a growl, "Suck me, now."

I bite down on his thumb, surprising him, and he pulls back with a hiss. I can't help but grin as his dark eyes narrow on me. "Fuck me, now."

"You sure you want to play this game, Snow Bunny?" he asks, hovering over me, our chests brushing with each breath. His fingers tangle in my hair, and he gives a sharp tug just as he slams into me.

The tears I held back from almost gagging spill over as I scream. He thrusts into me again, hitting the same spot, and the orgasm that washes over me is sudden and forceful. My whole body tightens as I cry out.

Asher licks my tears, groaning. "Your fucking tears are as delicious as your cunt." He grunts as his hips stutter, and I can feel his cum fill me. He gives my cheeks one last lick before whispering, "Change your mind, Snow Bunny?"

My brain is fuzzy, but I manage to mumble, "No."

He laughs and pulls out. "Wouldn't want you to give up too quickly."

I whimper when Alair moves in to take Ash's place. He hovers over me as he massages my chest. "I love your breasts."

I arch into him as he sucks a nipple into his mouth, then lets it go with a pop. He hovers over the other breast and says, "You are causing trouble, Little Fox."

"I thought you loved trouble," I reply breathlessly.

He snickers and sucks my other nipple into his mouth while slipping a finger into my cunt. He slides his finger in and out slowly before he releases my nipple with another pop. "I should make sure you're ready for Mir. He can be a bit greedy."

I'm about to ask what he means but gasp when his soaked finger caresses my ass. "Alair?" I groan.

"Flip her!" he orders. Before I know what's happening, I'm flipped over onto my stomach. My wrists are once again restrained, but my ass is now lifted in the air. I look over my shoulder to find that Ash and Mir are each holding one of my ankles.

Mir smacks my ass, making me squeal. "Such a plump ass. Her skin is pale and perfect for reddening."

I moan into the hard surface of the table as Alair teases my cunt with his cock. He circles my entrance as he runs his hands down my spine and back up. Slowly, he slides into me with a groan. "Shit, Little Fox. How are you still so tight?"

His thumb circles my ass, and I keen as I push back onto his thumb. With another groan, he pulls out, then slams back in. "So needy."

"I'm so close," I whine. I'm on the edge of another orgasm, and I want it so badly. His pace slows and I whimper, "Alair…"

"Mhm… I love the way you say my name, Little Fox. Beg for me."

I shake my head in refusal, and he stops thrusting completely, his thumb continuing to tease my ass. I feel the edges of my orgasm disappear, and I cry, "Alair!"

He chuckles and continues to thumb my ass, his cock not moving an inch. "Beg for it."

I tighten around his cock, hoping that will change his mind, but it doesn't. I scream in frustration, "Fuck me!"

He tsks. "Now, now. That sounds like a demand. Try again."

I whimper and push back, trying to force his cock deeper. "Fuck me, please."

He hums but just continues massaging the entrance to my ass. "That was better but still a demand. Polite demand but a demand nonetheless."

Tears of frustration burn my eyes as a desperate sob bubbles out of me. "Alair... make me come. Please make me come!"

He growls and pulls out. "Much better." He thrusts into me as he slips his thumb into my ass. I scream when stars explode behind my eyes. "Such a good Little Fox. Squeezing my cock so deliciously."

I feel him slip free, and I cry out. My hot breath fogging across the table. A hand slides over my ass, then gives it a soft pat. Mir growls, "I never imagined how arousing it would be to see my brothers' cum sliding down your legs. Dripping out of your needy cunt."

I mewl as I feel two fingers slip into me. He pumps a few times before making a scooping motion. I feel him slip his fingers between my cheeks and push the fluid into my ass. "Have to make sure you're ready for me, Darling."

He slowly slips his cock into my pussy with a groan. "Fuck... I'm not sure what I want to do more, fuck this warm, tight cunt or your sexy, tight ass."

He slaps my butt hard, and I come on command. I'm still sensitive from Alair. Mir squeezes my ass cheeks as I tighten around his cock, and he forces himself though my taut channel before slipping free.

His soaked cock circles my ass before he begins sliding in. I bite down on a scream, and tears stream down my face. I don't tell him to stop, though. Fuck, I don't tell him to stop because it feels too good. His piercings caress my inner walls in a completely new way.

Once he's buried to the hilt, he freezes. He rubs my ass before dragging his hands up and down my back. "Such a good job, Darling. You're doing so good. Taking my cock so beautifully."

I cry out as I push back onto him. I need more. I need so much more. He chuckles. "Very well, Darling." He slides out again before slowly pushing back in, picking up his pace when I don't tell him to stop. He's panting, and he continues to massage my ass cheeks.

I'm gulping down air as I feel warmth build in my core, the orgasm coming closer with each thrust. He slaps my ass, and I cry out, but it's not enough to send me over the edge. I'm so close. God, I'm so close. I feel the cool touch of darkness against my clit, and I know it's Mir trying to force an orgasm. It's still not enough, though.

"Mir..." I sob.

He growls, and the cold around my clit tightens. He pulls out and slams back into me while spanking both of my ass cheeks, hard. I keen as my pussy tightens around nothing. With a snarl, he comes inside of me. I feel my release spurt out, sliding down my thighs as he slowly pulls out.

Mir groans behind me as he runs a finger up my thighs to collect my release. I hear his satisfied hum and the pop of his finger being released from between his lips.

My vision is blurry and fingers tangle in my hair, forcing my eyes up. I meet Kasim's dark gaze as his fingers tighten. "I'm going to fuck that sassy mouth of yours, Princess."

My eyes hungrily take in the tattoos covering every inch of his skin. Ink swirls up his thighs and hips, merging to create new images across his abdomen and upper chest. Fingers caress my thighs as I feel a body settle behind me. Rev's deep voice rumbles as he says, "I'm going to fuck this dripping cunt. This table better be drenched by the time I'm done fucking you."

Kas caresses my bottom lip with the head of his cock and says, "Maybe between the two of us we can get you to change your mind."

Before I can reply, Kas slips his cock between my lips, and Rev slides into me. I moan around Kas's cock when I feel the caress of Rev's piercings. I am beginning to wish all these men had pierced cocks. It feels amazing. The two of them work together to fuck me, matching each other's pace, thrusting in and out in a steady rhythm. Kas pushes into my mouth as Rev slides out of my cunt.

Tears stream down my cheeks as I gag on Kas's cock, but he doesn't let it deter him. It seems to only fuel his need to fuck my mouth harder. His fingers tighten their grip in my hair, tugging the strands. "Gods, this fucking mouth. Fuck!"

I hum around his cock, and without warning, he lets out a roar, his cum shooting down my throat as I try to swallow it all down. The high I feel from making this grump of a man come has me tightening around Rev.

Rev's grip on my hips tightens, his knuckles practically white, as his hips stutter. He quickens his pace, and Kas slips out of my mouth. I look up, and he's smirking down at me. Drool and cum spill down my chin, and his eyes flare at the sight. "Bene, fuck her mouth."

I turn to find Bene smirking. "Does my dragoness want my cock?"

Licking my lips, I nod, and my voice is hoarse as I say, "Yes." Then Rev pinches my clit, making me moan.

I feel a thumb caress my bottom lip and force my eyes open to find Bene on his knees in front of me. He pushes his thumb inside my mouth, and I suck it as if it were his cock. His breath hitches, and he removes his thumb. "Open," he growls.

I open my mouth without argument, and he takes advantage. I close my lips around his cock, licking him like an ice cream cone before sucking again. Rev hits that amazing spot inside me again, and I groan.

Bene's fingers tangle in my hair and he says, "You were right, brother. Her mouth feels fucking amazing."

Rev pinches my clit, slamming into me, and I come again, screaming around Bene's cock. Rev grunts as he continues to thrust into my tight channel, and Bene picks up his pace fucking my mouth.

Rev slaps my ass as he grunts his release. My orgasm is not quite finished, and he somehow sends me into another by spanking my ass. The vibrations of my scream send Bene into an early orgasm, his cum dripping down my chin as he pulls out.

I've been fucked— thoroughly fucked—by seven men. I collapse forward onto the sticky table in exhaustion, my ass still up in the air as Rev slips out.

Rev grunts as he slides a thumb up my thigh, trying to capture our combined release. I feel him pressing it back inside me. His voice is thick as he says, "I want you full of our cum. Swollen with our release."

His thumb finally unplugs my entrance, and I feel a warm rag glide between my legs. All I can do is whimper as tears escape my tightly closed lids. I'm still so sensitive; I can only imagine how swollen I am. Dax gently wipes me down before lifting me up off the table and carrying me out of the room. His voice is soft as he says my name. "Eira?"

I hum, thoroughly fucked into a daze, as he continues down the hallway, heading for my room. He gently lays me on the bed before pulling the covers up over me. He crawls onto the bed, lying on his side next to me. With his elbow propping up his head, he asks, "Did we change your mind?"

I chuckle and force my eyes open. His eyes are back to their bright blue. Soft and tranquil. "No," I whisper.

He huffs out a sigh, looking away. "I didn't think so."

Rolling onto my side to face him, I pull a hand out of the covers to caress his cheek. He sighs, and his hand comes up to cover mine. I wait until Dax's eyes meet mine again to say, "I'll make you a deal."

He smiles softly. "What deal is that, Little Raven?"

"I won't fly away," I say. His eyes widen at the reference to his nickname for me. I shimmy on the bed, so I can be eye level with him. "I won't fly away, but you have to allow me to spread my wings. I won't stray too far."

His head falls forward, resting his forehead against mine. "Eira..."

"I will make sure I stay with you or one of the others at all times."

He closes his eyes, his face scrunching up as if tortured. When his eyes open again, they shimmer with emotion I've never seen from him before. "You will not stray far," he whispers firmly.

"I will not stray far. I promise."

"Very well," he huffs out, mumbling, "the others are going to kill me."

I snuggle into him, wrapping my arms around him. He's stiff for a moment before he relaxes, then embraces me. "They won't kill you," I say with a yawn.

"You do not know your worth, Little Raven. We would all kill for you."

I yawn again, closing my eyes. "If you say so."

CHAPTER TWENTY-THREE

S hit. Shit, Shit, Shit, Shit, SHIT! I fucked up. Oh... I really fucked up. There was one rule. *One* fucking rule. And as long as I agreed to that rule, I was allowed to join the others on the battlefield. Stick to one of the guys at all times like glue, and *do not* find myself alone. Easy, right?

Well, I somehow found myself smack in the middle of the battle with not a single one of my men in sight. *Shit.* I frantically look around, hoping to spot them, as I continue to fend off the king's men. I am not strong enough to cut them down to defend the land.

Blood and gore surround me no matter which way I turn. I need to remember that these are no longer the people of my kingdom. Most of them have been turned into the undead that the king uses to do his bidding and invade lands. There are a few who are still alive, but they have been corrupted by the king's propaganda. With promises of power they will never gain clouding their mind.

I finally see one of the guys. Kas. Kas! Of all of the guys to find, of course, it had to be him. He is going to be so mad.

A glint out of the corner of my eye forces me to turn and block a sword coming down on me fast. I'm so distracted by trying to push him away that I don't notice the male who sneaks up behind me. I let out a screech as my hair is snatched in someone's fist. I try to swing around, but a large arm encircles me as my hair is tugged harder.

The male behind me yells, "Halt!"

The undead instantly pause around us. A cold chill rushes down my spine at how quickly they obeyed. Is he somehow in control of the undead? He yells again, "I have the princess! Let us return to the king!"

A voice rings out among the horde of soldiers. "Unhand her now."

No. No! Of all of the guys to find me like this it had to be him? Where did he come from? I'd only seen Kas. I want to scream *Dax don't make yourself known!*

My hair is yanked again, and I struggle against the asshole holding me. He growls in my ear, "Settle, Princess. The king never said we had to bring you back alive."

My eyes widen, and I see Dax move into view. All I can do is silently beg him to shut up. His father doesn't know he is trying to take the throne. I watch as he marches through the soldiers, his armor glistening red. His eyes meet mine briefly, then shift to the man holding me. "Release the girl, now."

The man behind me chuckles darkly. "What makes you think you can give me orders?"

I silently plead for Dax to look at me. *Please. Please look at me. Don't tell him who you are. Don't do it for me.* But he ignores me and says, "I am Prince Dax of the Kingdom Wylan, son of King Balor. I am your Prince! Now, release the girl."

I feel the man shift behind me, and I can only imagine him cocking his head to the side when he asks, "Is that so?" He lets out a bellowing laugh before he replies, "Traitor to the king. Kill him."

Everything happens between one blink and the next. With unnatural speed, an undead man steps up behind Dax and spears him straight through the abdomen.

I can't stop the scream that erupts from me as I watch blood seep from the wound. He coughs, a spray of red coating his lips and chin. His eyes meet mine, and he gives me a sad smile. "Don't worry, Little Raven. I'll find you again."

I shake my head as I scream and writhe in the man's grasp, but he drags me away. Away from the man now dying because of me. The man I once thought was nothing but a villainous prince. All I can do is watch as the undead, unconcerned with Dax's army, trail behind us as I'm carried away. Through the gaps in bodies, I see the others close in around Dax.

They quickly grab him and rush back to the castle. I catch a brief look from Kas when he looks over his shoulder in my direction. I can see it, the indecisive look in his eyes as he debates whether to come after me or stay with Dax.

I shake my head as tears fall from my eyes. I know he can't hear my whispered words, but I hope he understands anyway. "Go. Save him."

His eyes narrow, but he gives me a sharp nod, then disappears from view as bodies close in. I'm thrown over someone's shoulder and carried off like a sack of potatoes. I don't fight, what would be the point? I can't fight off all these men. And the only men who could, are too busy trying to save Dax.

My head bounces, and I close my eyes as my tears slide into my hair from being carried upside down. My nose is now clogged, so I have to breathe through my mouth. The man holding me slaps my thigh, growling, "Stop blubbering, it's irritating."

The tears won't stop, though. No matter how hard I bite my lip, I can't force the pain to override my need to cry. The tears won't stop.

I'm flipped upright again and thrown into a carriage, my head painfully smacking against the floor. But even that pain doesn't override the crater in my chest. The door is slammed shut behind me, and I hear the man complaining. "I hate crying women."

Safe within the confines of the carriage, I break. There's no longer any point in trying to hold in my cries. So... I let it go. I sob and sob as I curl into a ball. Sobbing to the point of hiccupping, I scream, "I hate you!"

I *hate* him. I *hate* all of them. They made me care. Made me feel things I'd never felt. Cherished. Needed. *Loved.*

I scream again as I thump a fist against the floor of the carriage. How dare they! How fucking dare they! They are villains. But... that isn't really how I feel. They never felt like villains even after what I saw. The only evil thing they did was steal my most precious possession.

My heart.

The problem? I don't know if I had stolen theirs. And now, I'm not sure I'll ever find out.

I thump my head against the floor until I can feel myself getting dizzy. I give my head one last hard thump against the carriage floor, sending myself to meet the darkness. The dark is better than the utter agony I feel with each beat of my heart.

Maybe I'll find Rev in the dark. If so... I never want to wake up. *Please. Please death, take me. Death would be a mercy at this point. Allow me this mercy.*

I didn't die. No, unfortunately, I woke up to the smiling monster I wished to never see again. I must have done something terrible in a past life because the gods have never smiled upon me. No, only villains deserve this treatment.

He grins down as he reaches for me. "Come, Little Snowflake. I've missed you."

I shake my head as I push myself against the opposite wall of the carriage. I press as close as I can, hoping to meld with the wood. To disappear.

He impatiently clicks his tongue and holds out a hand. "Now, now. You know how I hate to wait."

Tears gather in my eyes. The one thing I promised never to do in front of this man was cry, but I can't stop it. I choke on a sob, and he snaps out a hand, grabbing my ankle. I kick at his hand, but his grip is too tight.

He laughs. "Oh, I will love breaking you again, pet."

He drags me out of the carriage kicking and screaming. His pace is quick as he takes me to the castle. He barges into his room and pins me on his bed. "Chain her up!" he orders.

A few of his men come into the room and circle around us. My hands are pulled, and shackles are placed on my wrists. My heart quickens when I hear the click of them locking around not only my wrists but my ankles too.

I'm positioned spread eagle as the king rises and shifts off the bed. He stares down at me with his disgusting mirrored black pits for eyes. Darkness gathers around him as he demands, "Leave me to my prize."

I tremble as I watch his men obey, and I'm left helpless at the king's mercy again. He licks his lips as he strips off his clothes, his cock springing to life. He grabs a knife from the floor before moving toward me again. Slipping the blade between my breasts, he wastes no time in cutting my shirt off me.

The men who dragged me here had stripped me of my armor, so I was left with only my shirt and pants. I hadn't bothered with undergarments this morning, but I wished for them now.

He licks his lips as he cuts off my pants, leaving me completely bared before him. I shrink into the bed as his fingers caress the scars he had given me. The scars Dax had made his own.

"Your skin slices so beautifully," he says hoarsely. He slides off the bed, looking around the room. I quickly do the same myself and find a large mirror above me as well as several others placed around the room. When my eyes find the king again, they widen, and my heart starts to race. He pulls a whip off the wall, then walks over to me. He taps it in his palm as his eyes meet mine.

"Knives are my favorite, Little Snowflake. But I have hungered for your screams ever since I heard how you screamed for my son." The sound of glass breaking makes me look up to find the mirror above me melding into tentacles.

My wide eyes turn to him as I beg, "Please... please don't."

"Hmm, you beg so beautifully too. Can I make you scream and beg me to stop?" He taps the whip in his palm once more before letting it unravel. The darkness in the room flares as he pulls his arm back. "Let's see if I can break you."

The moment he yanks his arm back, the tentacles reach out and squeeze my breasts. Each snap of the whip against my skin makes me scream until my voice is hoarse. The king's breathing grows heavier with each of my screams. Tears stream down my face as the tentacles caress my skin. It's not loving or pleasurable like my men. The touch is cold and harsh as the tentacles slip between my legs. "Stop!" I beg as a hiccup slips between my lips.

He pauses for a moment, and I look down to find the head of his cock dripping with pre-cum. It looks like one simple touch will have him exploding. His chest is rapidly rising and falling, while his eyes take in the bloody mess he's made of my body, and the tentacles in between my legs. He groans. "Beg. Beg me to stop."

I don't hesitate as I sob, "Please, stop!"

I watch as he runs his hand down to squeeze his cock, pumping it a few times. "I hope my son is dead," he says as he pants with excitement, "then I'll get to keep you."

With one hand he's painfully squeezing his cock as he pumps. With the other, he rears back with the whip. The moment it slices my bruised and broken body covered in welts, he roars out his release. I can't do anything but sob while he pumps himself until he lets out a satisfied grunt. "No one here is allowed to touch that cunt, except for me. You are mine. My men had their fun with you before, but now you are my toy and mine alone."

I cry harder when I feel his finger slip inside me. "This cunt is mine now, Little Snowflake."

CHAPTER TWENTY-FOUR

I sit chained to the floor, feeling as though I'm in a daze. I think it's been weeks since the battle, but it is impossible to tell time here. I've been placed on the ground right next to the king's throne, so he can keep an eye on me. I'm once again without clothes. He says it's so he can enjoy my body. But I think it's because he likes seeing the marks he leaves behind. He also refuses to feed me adequately. I am fed only enough to keep me alive but weak. The terror of not knowing what happened back in Wylan makes it hard to stomach food. When I do try, the food sits like lead in my stomach. I often end up vomiting after my sessions with the king anyways.

I wince as I try to situate myself in a more suitable position. My knees ache from kneeling so long on the hard floor. Though, to be honest, my whole body aches. Every inch. The king wants me kept in eyesight at all times. He doesn't want one of his men thinking they can play with his toy.

The king seems hopeful that his son is dead since he has not attempted to retrieve me. He had said the healers of Wylan would most likely have been able to save Dax, and if they did, he would enjoy playing the game with his son. That's all this is to him, a game. A game of chess, and he is waiting to see what move his son will make next. He doesn't seem to care that his son wants to take over the kingdom. He definitely doesn't care about the thousands of people who have died. He's focused only on the game. A tug-of-war fight over the toy.

The king has shown his cowardice in this war. He won't fight for the kingdom; he would rather turn its people into undead minions who will do his dirty work and fight for him. I grunt as I try to shift again to relieve some of the pain in my knees. I hear a laugh behind me and look over my shoulder to find the king smiling down at me.

"Do you like your new position, Snowflake?"

I grind my teeth as I say, "Yes, Your Highness." During my time here, I've learned that if I am agreeable, he won't drag me back to his torture room. The last time he took me there, he had threated to fuck the attitude out of me. I haven't been back to that room since. And there is no way I am going to willingly let this man rape me.

"Are you still hoping for my son to save you?" he taunts with a laugh.

I turn and look toward the door. Dax's last words continue to haunt me. *I'll find you.* No, I gave up hope for that days ago. As much as the king boasts how the healers would have saved him, I'm sure Dax is dead. The others would stay by his side until they marched their army here for revenge. They would not come to save a woman they mildly care for. Not when they could kill the king. No. I stopped hoping because it hurts too much to think I meant nothing to them. I don't blame them though. They are the villains after all. My life is miniscule compared to gaining the power to control the kingdoms.

It hurts a little to think about, but I understand it. I had called them horrible names and used them for my own pleasure. I let out a huff, wincing a little when I sit too hard on my bruised knees.

"I think we should have one of our sessions this evening. Would you like that, Snowflake?"

I bow my head in submission as I respond, "Of course, Your High-ness." The last thing I want is a session with the king, but if I argue or act as though being with him is distasteful, it will be much worse for me. The beatings will be worse, and he will allow the tentacles from the mirror to touch me as well.

He stands, making his way over to me. His fingers slip into my hair and tug hard, making me wince. My head is still sore from when I slammed it against the floor of the carriage. He leans down right in front of my face. "I wonder if you'd fight me if I kissed you."

I choke down the vomit that's building as I press my lips tightly together. He laughs at my reaction and releases his grip on my hair. Returning to his throne, he grins. "Once I've broken you completely, I will kiss you."

Outside of the throne room, I can hear the guards start yelling, which startles me.

"What is going on?" the king demands, yelling at his men for an-swers as he looks to the doors to the throne room.

A roar sounds outside the doors and someone barks, "Where is she?" The doors to the throne room are slammed open, and I'm stunned. Completely frozen in place. Eyes wide, I gape at the hand-some man striding down the aisle toward the throne, carrying a blood-soaked sword, looking like death reincarnate. Angry, black shadows swirl around him, but his dark eyes never once leave the king. Peering behind him briefly, I'm stunned to find six other familiar faces. They... they came...

I struggle to hold back a sob as I watch the prince walk toward us. He moves like the reaper of souls, swinging his sword at anyone who gets in his way. Finally, he pauses in front of the king and me. When he looks down at me, I watch the darkness in his eyes flicker, giving me a quick glimpse of his bright blue eyes before they turn black again. Then he turns his dark eyes to meet the king.

I watch, mouth agape, as he points the sword at his father. "You will not touch her ever again," he states, his voice cold as ice. "I warned you that I would not share. She is *MINE*. I should kill you where you stand for touching her after I gave you such a gracious warning."

I shiver at the possessiveness I hear in his words. He has called me his so many times, but at this moment, I believe him. I believe I belong to him. He cares for me just as much as I care for him. My heart flutters at the thought that, maybe, just maybe, I had stolen his heart like he had stolen mine.

I let out a very undignified squeak when his sword slams down on the wooden anchor attaching my chains to the floor. He covers me with his cape, and I wince when he slips an arm around my waist and heaves me up. The cold kiss of his darkness caresses my skin and makes me shiver. He presses his face into my neck and takes a deep breath, calming the dark swirls, but his eyes are still inky black pits as they lift to meet the king's.

The king is grinding his teeth but doesn't move as we slowly back away, walking backward, so we don't give the king an opportunity to stab us in the back like the coward he is. The others surround Dax and I as we hastily exit the throne room. Dax's shadows disappear, and I sigh, not caring to look at the king anymore. I'm safe now within Dax's arms. I burrow deeper into his chest, trying to soak in his now-warm body. I never thought I would be so happy to see him.

"You are playing a dangerous game, son," the king yells from atop his throne.

As we step out of the room, I hear a rumble in Dax's chest, then he growls and says, "And you broke the rules the moment you touched what is *mine*. You'd do well to remember my warning. *Mine*."

I try to keep the tornado of emotions fighting inside me from slipping out until we are safely out of the castle. The moment I see sunshine and can breathe in the fresh air again, I bury my face into his neck and sob. "You're alive," I whisper once I've calmed a bit.

His hold on me tightens as he briskly walks down the cobblestone path. "Of course, I'm alive." He clears his throat as if to banish the darkness, trying to lighten his next words with a half chuckle. "I did not think you would care if I lived or died. Though, your scream on the battlefield convinced me otherwise."

"I watched that man plunge a sword through you!" I cry.

"Yes, well we have amazing healers. I am well."

My hand lowers, and I cover the spot where he was stabbed. Where I would expect puckered skin or even bandages, solid muscle meets my hand instead. "You are well?" I whisper.

He gives me a quick nod and says, "You can do a thorough search, if you must, once we get home."

"Home," I repeat through my tears.

His now bright blue eyes find mine as he says, "Back to Wylan, of course."

I've never thought much about Wylan being home. But right now, it's the only place I want to be. I nod as I smile through my tears. "Please, take me home."

Chapter Twenty-Five

The ride back to Wylan with my injuries was rough, but we finally made it safely to the castle. Dax marches through the front doors, not stopping for a moment. "Dax?" I say quietly.

He grunts and continues his quick pace through the halls.

"Dax?" I ask again louder.

"Yes?" he grunts out.

"Where are we going?"

His eyes narrow, but he continues to look forward. "To the healers."

My eyes widen. "Why are we going to the healers? Are you alright? Did you push yourself too much?"

"We are going for you, Eira!" he yells, making me wince. His eyes turn to dark black pits again as darkness fills the hallway. He pauses to take several deep breaths, and the darkness slowly begins to dissipate with each breath he takes. With one last deep breath, he continues down the hall. His voice is softer now as he says, "Forgive me. My anger got away from me."

"It's alright," I say softly. "I do not need to see the healer, Dax. I am fine."

He freezes, and his grip on me tightens. "You believe you do not need to see the healer?"

I look up at him to find him frowning down at me. I arch a brow. "I am fine, Dax."

He lowers me, so my legs touch the ground, and I can stand on my own. I pull his cape tighter around myself as I find seven sets of eyes staring at me. He steps away, and I watch his fingers curl into fists. "You think yourself well enough?"

I shrug. "I'm fine. I do not wish to bother the healers when they have better things to do." In truth, I don't want any more foreign hands touching me. I don't want anyone touching me other than my men.

"You think yourself a bother," Kas states and growls.

My brows furrow, and I shake my head. "I did not say that, Kas." How can I tell them what's wrong without admitting what the king did to me? The nightmare of being forced back to that castle after escaping it once.

"Then what are you saying?" Rev asks with a frown.

I huff out a sigh and try to explain, "I am sure there are others who need the healers more than me. I also…"

I let out a squeak when the cape is ripped from my body. I am now completely bare, and Ash holds the cape. His eyes narrow on me as he angrily huffs. "You believe your body is less important than anyone else's?"

Bene points at Dax as he glares at me. "We had to hold our prince down, so he could heal."

Before I can say anything more, Mir snaps, "We have been going insane around here waiting for him to heal enough to come for you! He would have gone after you still *bleeding* if we didn't stop him!"

I try to say something again, but Alair interrupts me this time. "You think you're so replaceable that we would allow you to skip seeing the healers?"

"That isn't what I said!" I yell before anyone else can interrupt me. I'm frustrated and feeling so overwhelmed with them acting like they... well, like they love me. I simply don't want anyone touching me! I shiver at the thought of foreign hands on my skin. Wait... My thoughts start to spiral as I try to understand why they would be acting like this. Do they love me? Is that possible? My eyes widen when they meet Dax's bottomless, dark pits. I can't stop myself from asking, "Do you love me?"

His eyes widen for a moment before narrowing again, but he remains quiet, which sparks my irritation. It's better than the fear of foreign hands touching me, though. "Do you even know what love is, Dax?"

He grunts as he answers, "No. No, I do not. But I know what I feel. I know what I have felt with you missing the last few weeks."

Standing completely naked in the hallway in front of these men like this makes me feel vulnerable. My fresh wounds from the king are on full display, but I get a feeling Dax feels the same way fully clothed. I remember our first fight when I wanted freedom. He had told me he had an obsidian heart. So, I decide to push. "And what did you feel, Dax? What could you possibly feel in that obsidian heart of yours?"

He thumps a fist against his chest over his heart as he says, "I feel as though I would tear the world apart if anything were to happen to you." He raises his voice as he continues, "I feel as if I would tear the very fabric between life and death to steal you away!" His fingers spread over his chest before tightening into fists again. He's breathing heavily while the darkness swirls around us. His emotions are too much for him to contain. "I would... I would steal you from death himself if you were to try and leave this world."

Taken aback by his confession, I step closer to him. "Is that... is that what love is to you?" I ask quietly.

He stares at me, his eyes like bottomless pools of ink. "I don't know," he whispers.

And that is the moment I finally figured him out. His obsidian heart is as fragile as glass. It would break into thousands of shards... for me. If I tried to put it back together, it would cut me so deeply—so thoroughly—that pieces of him would forever be embedded. Forever a part of me... And that scares me. Because this is bigger than love. But as I watch him now, his body vibrating with emotions he isn't sure how to process, I realize that this is his version of love. He loves me but doesn't know how to voice it.

I take another step forward and reach for him. I caress his cheek, and his eyes close. Resting my trembling hand against his chest, I whisper, "Tell me."

"Eira..." he pleads.

"Tell me what you are holding back." I can see it. In the depths of his dark eyes, I can see he's holding something back.

His hand engulfs the one I have against his cheek. His whispered words are almost too soft for me to hear. "You are my obsession. My everything. I would kill for you... bleed for you. I would capture you within a cage, Little Raven. To keep you forever."

I can't help but smile as I rise on my tiptoes to brush my lips against his. Pulling away, I chuckle softly. "So you missed me?" I tease.

He groans and glares at me. "Must you always be so difficult?"

I shrug as I step away. Turning to Ash, I see him holding out a hand for me. "May I have the cape back now?"

He arches a brow. "Will you go to the healers?"

Groaning, I nod. I clearly am not going to get out of a trip to the healers, but maybe having them with me will help settle some of my unease. "Okay, I'll go to the healers."

He takes a step closer to me and wraps the cloth around my body. He stays there for a moment, staring down at me. I arch a brow in question. "Do you have something to say, Ash?"

His brows knit as he continues to stare. Worried about my happy-go-lucky man turning grumpy on me, I reach for his hand. Threading my fingers through his, I give it a squeeze. "Ash?"

His eyes jump to Dax before meeting mine. "I... I..."

I tug on his hand again as I begin to walk. "Walk me to the healers." He nods and follows. I have a feeling he needs to speak to me but doesn't want the others around. I look over my shoulder to find them still watching us. I yell, "I'll meet you all in my room."

They hesitate for a moment but seem to take the hint and begin heading in the opposite direction. I huff out a sigh as we turn the corner. I'm about to ask Ash what's wrong when I'm unexpectedly engulfed in his arms.

I wince at the suddenness of it, but wrap my arms around him, so he doesn't pull away. His voice is muffled when he grumbles, "I told you not to run."

I hold him close. "I knew you would chase me."

His grip on me tightens as he mumbles into my neck, "I will chase you forever, Snow Bunny. You are my greatest hunt."

I grin when I realize this is his way of saying 'I love you'. My chest tightens, and I whisper back, "I hope so."

He pulls away with a soft smile on his lips. "Let's get you looked at. I don't like seeing all those wounds unless they are from one of us."

CHAPTER TWENTY- SIX

Now I know I shouldn't be walking around the castle by myself... at night... when I've finally returned. But food. I'm so hungry! I tiptoe down the hallway, the guards giving me arched brows as I pass.

I didn't want to bother any of the guys, considering the dark circles under their eyes. I'm sure this is the first time they have slept since Dax was stabbed, and I was taken.

My foot hits a creaky board, and I hiss, "Fuck." I wait for a few moments to pass before quietly continuing my walk.

I stiffen when a guard asks louder than I wish, "What are you doing, miss?"

I press my finger to my lips and shush him. "Shh! I'm trying to be quiet here."

He rolls his eyes, asking again, "What are you doing?"

My eyes narrow. "I'm getting food. Now be quiet, so I can be stealthy."

"You should be guarded, miss," he insists.

Growling, I point up and down the hallway. "There are guards all the way to the kitchen. I am guarded. Now, if you would kindly shut the fuck up, so I can sneak that would be grand."

I turn to continue my stealthy mission when I hear the squeak of a door opening. *Damnit.* My shoulders slump when I hear my name. "Eira?"

Turning around, I find Rev with his head poking out the doorway. He looks up and down the hall, his sleepy eyes meeting mine. He arches a brow. "What are you doing?"

I shoot the noisy guard a death glare before softening my gaze for Rev. "I was *trying* to walk quietly, so I didn't wake you."

He hums, rubbing his face sleepily, as he steps out of his room. "Then, I'll escort you."

I shake my head. "No, It's okay. Go back to bed."

He gives me a soft smile but continues my way. "I will not be able to sleep now, knowing you are out and about without one of us by your side."

I send the guard another glare when Rev steps up to my side. He offers me his arm, and I gladly take it. "I'm sorry I woke you. I'm hungry and wanted a snack."

"You could have woken one of us to take you. We do not mind."

Laying my head against his bicep, we slowly walk to the kitchen side by side. "I know, but you all looked exhausted. I wanted to make sure you slept."

He softly replies, "That was very kind of you, Sunshine." He ushers me onto a chair. "What would you like to eat?"

"Anything," I say happily. I am not about to be picky. I'm famished. After weeks of not being properly fed by the king, I will eat anything Rev puts in front of me.

He arches a brow before turning to grab a few things from the storage area. I notice he grabs some of the leftover stew we had for dinner as well as a few rolls. He places it all in front of me, and I don't hesitate to dig in.

My mouth is full when he reaches behind him, then presents me with an apple dessert. I grin as I finish off my stew and rolls, followed by immediately digging into the dessert. I point my fork at him as I finish my bite. "How is my shadow doing?"

He arches a brow. "Your shadow?"

I grin and pop another bite into my mouth. "Mhm."

He smiles as he leans onto his elbows. "Not sure I can be your shadow when I no longer spend much time in the shadows, Sunshine."

"Why is that?" I ask through another bite.

He shrugs. "Well, I have my Sunshine now."

My grin widens. "Is that so?"

Rev leans over the counter to press a kiss to my forehead. When he pulls away, his dark brown eyes meet mine. "You are the glow that draws me out of the shadows. You are my light, my Sunshine."

"Do you wish you were in the shadows?" I whisper.

His eyes roam over my face before he murmurs, "Not anymore."

The morning light streams through the cracks of the curtains, sending beams of sunlight throughout my room. With a yawn, I stretch, groaning when it makes every ache in my body known. The healers did an amazing job, but they are only able to use so much magic. Most of their magic went to saving Dax.

Either way, I am grateful for the healing that they were able to do, even if it left more scars behind. Dax was furious when he discovered that not all of my injuries had healed. I told him that magic could only do so much, and I didn't mind healing the old-fashioned way.

I sit up with a groan and huff out a heavy sigh. I rub my eyes to clear the sleep from them but let out a loud screech when they finally focus.

Mir is holding up both hands, and his face turns red. "Sorry! I didn't mean to frighten you!"

Plopping back down on the bed, I hold a hand over my rapidly beating heart. "You frightened me half to death, Branimir!"

He rushes over in a panic. "I'm sorry! So sorry, Eira!"

"Good heavens, what did you think would happen when I found a man hiding in the corner of my room just staring at me? That would frighten anyone!"

He groans and covers his face, but that doesn't hide his bright red ears. "Forgive me, Darling!"

I swat him as I huff out, "Announce yourself next time, or better yet don't hide in the corner like some weirdo!"

"I'm sorry," he whines in embarrassment.

"Now, if you are done creeping on me from the corner like a weird stalker..." I grumble as I shift on the bed to make room and pat the spot next to me. "Lie down. I'm assuming you wanted to spend time with me?"

He nods, his hands still covering his face. I pat the bed again and whine, "Lie down with me."

He huffs, uncovering his face. Which is still bright red when he shifts onto the bed to lie next to me. He holds himself deathly still, and I groan, "I will not break, Mir. You can move closer."

"I do not wish to hurt you," he whispers.

"I find it hard to believe you would hurt me. Now, hold my hand before I get offended."

He moves a bit closer before slipping his hand into mine. Our fingers tangle together, and his hold is gentle. Too soft for him. I tighten my grip on his hand. "Mir, I won't break. Your bite hurts more than your hand holding."

He snorts a laugh before groaning. "Please, do not mention biting you. It just makes me want to fuck you."

I laugh. "Then fuck me."

He sighs. "Not yet, Darling. You need to heal a bit more."

"I do hope you are still hungry when that time comes," I joke.

His grip in mine tightens, and his tone turns serious. "I'll always need you. My hunger for you will never die."

I hum as I snuggle closer to him. I'm finding that my men may not know how to say 'I love you' with words, but their actions speak for themselves. It's just not in the 'normal' way. But we aren't normal people. And even though I know I care deeply for them, I'm still too scared to say it myself.

As I wake, I spread out my arms but feel only a chill. Slowly opening my eyes, I see Mir is no longer beside me. With a groan, I get out of bed and glance out the window to see that the sun has made it over the horizon. The guys will all be at training, which means I will get a few hours of alone time.

I look around the room and ponder what to do with the few hours I have alone. I'm sure once the guys finish training that they will seek me out. I don't feel like walking to the library, but I do have some books stashed in the corner.

Maybe I should make a reading nook, or better yet a reading burrow, somewhere I can store my Dragoness' hoard. I grin when I think of Alair's nickname for me. A burrow for his little fox. Biting my lip, I debate how to go about making myself a burrow.

I jump into action as the idea solidifies in my mind. I'll need lots of blankets. Opening the door to my room, I look down the hallway and find a few guards, but not a single one of my guys is in sight. Grinning, I run down the hall to Rev's bedroom.

I rush in and snatch a few of his blankets from his bed before taking off again. As I race back to my room, some of the guards give me looks with raised brows. I offer them a smirk as I toss the blankets onto my bed and head back out for more. Next up, Mir's bedroom.

I repeat this with each of the guys' rooms, and I now have a big pile on my bed. The guards grow curious the longer they watch me and have moved closer to my door to peer inside. One of them offers me an arched brow as I walk to the door to close it. "What are you planning with all of those blankets, miss?"

I grin as I answer, "I'm making myself a reading burrow. Have a nice day!" I shut the door with a huff of laughter. After looking at the blankets, I start to make myself a hidey hole. I lay blankets over the headboard and connect them to the footboard, then slide under the flaps on the side of the bed and burrow beneath the rest of my stolen blankets.

I can't help but grin at my pile of books by the headboard. Picking one at random, I begin to read as I relax under the blankets' warmth, while the comforting smell of my men wraps around me. Being surrounded by their scents adds an extra layer of safety and calm.

I'm halfway through my book when there's a knock at my door. "Come in," I yell from my position.

I hear the door slowly open, and a familiar voice rings out. "Eira? I know you've been cooped up in this room, I was wondering..."

Alair's voice trails off, and I can't help but smirk as I hear the question in his voice. "What have you done in here, Little Fox?"

I chuckle as I shuffle out of my burrowed spot on the bed and peek outside my makeshift hidey hole. I can see him looking over all of the blankets before his eyes meet mine. They are filled with amusement as I reply, "I made myself a reading burrow."

He snorts a laugh as he asks, "Do you mind if I join you?"

I nod as I slide back into my previous spot. It takes him a moment, but then he slides in next to me. I'm lying on my side, my book now forgotten, as he lies down on his side, propping himself up on one elbow while facing me.

"How was training?" I ask, noticing a few new scrapes on his face.

He shrugs. "Same as usual." He points toward my hoard of books. "What were you reading?"

With a smirk, I reply, "It seems I picked up a random book on the flora and fauna of the kingdom. I wasn't expecting it to be as interesting as it is."

He hums as he continues to stare at me. I can't help but reach up and gently caress his cheek before brushing his short ebon hair off his forehead. A few strands look to have curled from sweat.

His eyes flutter closed, and his breath hitches at my touch. "Did you read anything about foxes?" he whispers.

I continue to brush my fingers through his short locks as I reply, "I didn't get to the part about foxes. I don't know a lot about them, so I'm looking forward to learning about them."

His light hazel eyes pop open to reveal so much emotion hidden in their depths; I can't stop the soft gasp that escapes me. His voice is hushed as if this is a secret between the two of us. "Did you know that foxes mate for life?"

I shake my head no, however, the sentiment brings a smile to my face. There aren't many animals that create that type of bond. He wraps his fingers around my wrist and lifts my hand to cup his cheek.

"Foxes mate for life, Eira. You're *MY* Little Fox. Forever mine. I've captured the fox, but the fox has captured my heart," he admits quietly within our burrow of blankets. I lean forward, pressing my lips to his in a gentle kiss before pulling away. My thumb caresses his cheek as I say, "Then I will guard your heart, Alair. I promise I'll keep it safe, always."

CHAPTER TWENTY-SEVEN

I've managed to sneak all the way to the library without the guards ratting me out or one of the guys finding me. A few days have passed since I returned, and I'm feeling much better. But the guys still think I need to rest, so I've been stuck in my bedroom for days.

I'm going stir crazy! Hence why I waited till the guys left for training to sneak through the castle. I push open the library door and slip inside, closing the door softly behind me.

With a grin, I rush over to my pile of books, excited to dive into a fantasy world. I found a book about dragons, and it has sucked me in. Snuggling into the sofa, I pull my fluffy blanket over me. Opening the book to where I left off, I begin reading about dragons and magic.

My book suddenly goes flying across the room, and I screech when I hear my name behind me. I was so distracted with the book; I didn't hear anyone come in. "Merciful Goddess!" I yell as I look over my shoulder to find a wide-eyed Bene.

He's still standing in the doorway of the library, frozen mid-step. "Forgive me, Eira. I didn't realize that would frighten you."

My head falls back, and I look up at the ceiling. "I have found you men to be far more silent than necessary."

His face hovers over mine as his warm eyes stare down at me, filled with concern. "I will make noise next time. Are you well?"

I sigh as I nod. "I am, Bene." I lift my head to look for the casualty of my fright. I hope I didn't harm the book.

Bene holds the book with a soft smile as he comes around the sofa. "Your book, Little Dragoness."

I grin as I take it from him. Looking it over, the edges are a bit dinged from landing on the floor, but otherwise it looks fine enough. Holding it to my chest, I look up at Bene with a smile. "How did training go?"

He shrugs. "As well as training usually goes."

I hum as I pat the spot beside me. "Join me?"

He smiles and sits next to me. I shift around, so I can lie on the sofa with my head in his lap. "Getting comfortable?" he teases.

"Mhm. I want to continue reading, and you are the best pillow."

He chuckles and begins playing with my hair. I let out a content sigh as I open my book again. His voice is soft when he asks, "What are you reading?"

"A book about dragons and magic. It has become my favorite to read."

He hums as he says, "I find it hard to believe you have a favorite with a hoard as large as yours."

I shift my gaze from my book to his eyes. With an arched brow, I ask, "Do you not have a favorite book?"

He smirks. "I have a favorite book."

My eyes widen with excitement at gaining this knowledge. "What is it?"

His eyes roam over my face for a moment before meeting mine. "You."

My brows knit in confusion. "Me?"

He slides a hand from my hair to caress my cheek. "You are the novel readers desperately search for. A once in a lifetime kind of work. I never wish to stop reading you. Forever caressing your pages. My precious book."

My eyes widen at his confession before they soften. "I believe that will be a very long book, Bene. Do you really want to read the same story for so long?"

He smiles as he answers, "Each chapter is just as precious as the last. The story is built with each word written. I can't wait to turn the page to see what happens next."

"Is that right?"

He lowers to brush his lips across mine in a soft caress, then whispers, "It's a story I hope never ends."

"All stories must eventually come to an end," I whisper back.

He pulls away, and I see emotions I never thought I'd see in a villain's eyes. True fucking heartbreak. "Then I hope my story ends before yours."

My eyes burn. "Benedict…"

"Holding your closed book is unthinkable." He brushes his lips against mine and says softly, "Your book is the only one in my hoard."

The fear I felt about telling the others my feelings disappears in this moment. I can't fight my heart anymore. Book forgotten, I slip my fingers into his platinum locks. I press my lips to his, the kiss soft and languid. I pull away just enough for my lips to caress his as I tell him, "I love you. So let's end our stories together."

I should tell the others. I pace my room as I debate telling the others how I feel. We will be going into battle in a few days, and I don't want to go into it without them knowing how I feel. But would telling them cause them to change their minds and refuse my request to join them on the battlefield? Especially after what happened the last time.

My confession to Bene slipped between my lips before I could stop the words. I hadn't meant to tell him. But the wide-eyed look he gave me makes it hard to regret telling him. The way he ravished me on that sofa. Mhm. I feel heat pool between my legs just thinking about it.

Shaking myself out of the memory, I slap my face. *Focus!* Stop thinking about his dick and focus on the problem at hand. *What is the problem again?* The guys... Love! That's it. I was debating telling the others how I feel.

A knock at my door causes me to pause my pacing. Turning to the door, I say, "Yes?"

The door creaks open, and Dax pokes his head through. He looks pensive, which makes me worry. "Dax?"

With a huff, he slips into my room, closing the door behind him and leaning back against it. He's looking at the ground when he says, "I have bad news."

"I figured as much from your expression," I reply as I make my way over to him. I reach for his fisted hand and hold it in mine. "Dax? What's wrong?"

He allows me to take his hand into mine but refuses to look me in the eye. "It seems my father has decided that he is tired of waiting for me to make the next move."

I move so that he cannot escape my gaze as I state, "You still have not told me what is wrong."

His eyes bore into mine as he grunts. "He has assigned men to the border between Arcelia and Wylan. He is moving to attack."

My hands tighten around his before I nod. "Alright." I release his hands, turning to change into my battle leathers.

Before I get far, he grabs my arm. "Alright?"

I turn enough to meet his gaze. "Yes. Alright. Let's get ready to march out."

His grip on my arm tightens, and he growls out, "Eira, we are not ready. *You* are not ready. You haven't healed enough."

I turn fully to wrap my arms around him. He freezes at the sudden hug, but then slowly starts to relax. I squeeze him tighter as I say, "We are ready. Your men have been training every day. I have healed enough, Dax."

He wraps me tightly in his arms as grumbles, "You are not healed enough for my liking."

"The enemy will not wait for me to be at one hundred percent to attack. I am well enough to fight. I promise."

He pulls away, looking down at me with narrowed eyes. "You will not stray far from one of us."

It's a command not a request. I nod and smile. "I will not stray far."

His arms move from our embrace, so he can cup my face. His voice turning desperate as he begs, "Do not fly away, Little Raven."

"I will not fly away. I lo—" Before I can finish, he presses a finger to my lips. I arch a brow in question.

"Do not say it," he pleads. "Do not say it until this is over."

"Dax," I mumble behind his finger.

"An incentive, Little Raven." He moves his finger away to press a soft kiss against my lips. "A promise to come back to me."

CHAPTER TWENTY-EIGHT

It's as if every single one of my men agrees with Dax. The moment I go to tell them how I feel, they either cover my mouth with their hand or smash their lips to mine. Seems I won't be telling them how I feel before we leave for battle.

I'm buckling armor over my leathers when Kas steps in front of me. I feel his glare on me, and I can't help but smirk. "Do you wish to tell me something or by chance have a snarky remark before we head into battle?"

He doesn't say anything, just brushes my hand out of the way and takes over adjusting my armor. With my attention no longer on the straps, I look at my grumpy man. He's got a deep frown line between his brows as he concentrates.

I reach up and rub at the frown line between his brows. His eyes flick to me before returning to my buckles. "What, Princess?"

"Don't frown so much. Your face will get stuck like that."

He snorts and moves on to the buckles that secure my sword at my side. "This is my face. Do you find my face displeasing, Princess?"

I chuckle and shake my head. "I like your face very much."

The comment catches him off guard, and he freezes for a moment before his dark hazel eyes meet mine. "You... like my face?"

I grin. "Oh yes. Your face is very pleasing. Makes up for your shitty attitude."

It takes a moment, but a smirk slowly spreads across his face as turns his attention to the last of my straps. "Good to know."

I wait for him to finish before I punch him in the chest and run off. I yell over my shoulder, "Thank you! Still hate you!"

I hear him yell, "I'll hate you forever, Princess."

The way he says it makes me grin because he's just like the others. He can't say those three little words.

I run until I find Dax standing on the edge of a hill. It overlooks the valley between Wylan and Arcelia where the battle will take place. Stepping up beside him, I look out, and I see dark figures moving in the distance. The enemy and his undead army are making their way here.

I hadn't been nervous until now. But with each moment that passes, the figures grow closer and closer. My nerves grow as it starts to sink in that the battle is about to begin. A weight settles on my chest, and breathing becomes difficult as my nerves escalate.

"Are you with me, Little Raven?"

Choppy breaths escape my lips as I realize that it is time. This is what we have been training and planning for. Today is the day we take the kingdom or die trying. I have learned many things during my time with the prince. The Kingdom of Wylan has grown twisted and corrupt because of the king. It is no longer the land I remember seeing as a child. It has been forever changed, and I have a choice to make.

I can either hold onto old morals of a time that no longer exists or adapt and change. I can change the same way this land has. The heroes of old no longer make sense. Would a hero be willing to kill so many in order to save the few? Maybe. But a hero would never have risked his army to save me in the first place. I would have been written off as a casualty of war. Do I have the strength to change?

"Eira?"

My head jerks to Dax. His brows are knitted as his hard gaze meets mine. "Are you with me?"

I bite my lip and nod.

His eyes rove over my face before those icy blue orbs thaw. His gaze is soft as he cups my cheek. "You will forever and always be the light, the glow that will guide me home when I'm consumed by darkness. Do not smother your light, Little Raven. It is the only thing that guides us back to you."

My hand covers his as I huff out a breath. "I must change to belong in this new world."

I jump when I hear Kas step up behind me. "Would you ask the sun to stop shining?"

I roll my eyes as I reply, "No. But—"

He interrupts, "Would you ask the birds to stop singing?"

Looking over my shoulder, I say, "No. But Kas..."

He just arches a brow and talks over me. "Then why would you expect us to ask you to smother your radiance?"

Growling, I say, "You are not asking me to do anything. I am simply saying that I must change with the times to belong in this world."

Dax grips my jaw and forcefully turns my gaze to meet his. His icy expression returns as he frowns. "Who said you did not belong in this world?"

My breath catches as I force the words out, "This world."

His grip on my jaw tightens as he turns it to face the men I've grown to love. He growls and says, "You belong to them." He jerks my face back to him. "You belong to ME. That is all that matters. The world can burn to ash, for all I care. I will set this kingdom ablaze and make a new world if I must. Do I make myself clear?"

I nod as best I can with him still gripping my chin. A devilish grin appears on his face as he lowers himself enough so that he's at eye level with me. His grip loosens, and he caresses my bottom lip with his thumb. "Do I make myself clear, Little Raven?"

A shiver runs down my spine as I whisper, "Yes."

"Yes, what?" he asks, rubbing his thumb over my bottom lip, his gaze never wavering from mine.

My breath hitches, and I reply, "Yes, My Prince."

He groans as he shifts his grip back to my chin. He presses his lips to mine before nipping at my lip. Pulling away, he looks down at me with molten eyes. "Now, answer the previous question. Are you with me?"

"Yes," I reply without hesitation.

Chapter Twenty-Nine

All around me, the battle rages on. I'm covered in blood, but I've managed to stick by one of the guys at all times. And even though the enemy has tried to separate me from the others, I've managed to slip through their grasp.

I promised Dax that I would always stay next to one of them, and I won't break that promise. But I have managed to move slowly enough that whichever guy sticks with me hasn't noticed me moving closer to the king.

He was the first person I searched for when the battle started, and I've been trying to make my way in that direction ever since. I'm not sure how I managed to sneak as close to the king as I have, to be honest, but I have. I'm surprised neither his men nor mine have noticed me inching closer.

I'm shocked when I look over to find myself only a few feet from the king. This is my chance. Kas has fought to stay by my side the longest, and I quickly look to see where he is in my proximity. He's just at the outer limit of what would be considered too far, surrounded by men, and won't be able to keep me in his sight.

This is something I need to do, though. I am so close. I need to prove that I can be just as ruthless as my men and kill if necessary. I slowly make my way over to him using the stealth moves Kas taught me. The king doesn't have those odd tentacles around him, which is strange, but regardless, I can't lose this chance. I'm almost close enough to slide my knife across his throat when I feel a pinching pain in my back. I can only assume it's a knife. *Fuck.*

The king turns, offering me a malicious smile. The mirrored tentacles finally gather around him as he laughs. Over my shoulder, I catch a mirrored person form from the mirrored goo. It's not holding a knife, though, its hand is the knife. My attention is dragged back to the king when he says, "If you bow to me now, I will spare your life. My son has already chosen his side, but there is still time for you yet."

I shake my head and feel the knife dig further into my back, causing me to gasp out, "Never." I will never willingly go back to this man. I would rather spear myself on the knife at my back than ever think to agree to that.

He arches a brow as he steps closer. "Kings and Gods have bowed before me. What makes you think you can refuse for long? Come now, Little Snowflake. Bow."

I wait until he steps even closer before I say, "Kill me if you must, but I will never bow to a cowardly king who is proud to wear a crown studded with jewels symbolizing every life he has cut short. I will never bow to a king who wears the colors of the kingdoms he devoured."

The smell of iron and death surrounds me, but I refuse to let it make me lose my resolve and waver in what I must do. As quickly as Kas taught me, I spring forward and stab my knife directly into the king's throat. I grin when his eyes widen in surprise, and I use all my strength to lacerate as much tissue as I can, proving to him that underestimating me was a fatal mistake.

I hear a feminine sounding scream behind me, but I ignore it in favor of staring into the dying king's eyes. I gasp when I feel the sharp pain of a blade in my abdomen. Looking down, I see the king had his own blade ready, and it is now buried in my stomach. My eyes meet his as he begins to spit up blood.

His words are garbled as he says, "Taking... you... with... me."

I push him away, letting him fall, as I try to stay standing. He lands in a puddle of mirrored goo, and I watch as his body is slowly consumed by the liquid. *Odd* is the only thought that streaks through my mind when a feminine voice whispers in my head. I can't make out anything she's saying, so I try to block it out. I don't want to hear her; I need to get to my men.

I don't have the strength to look behind me for Kas. My eyes scan the distance, and without fail, they find Dax. His are wide as they take me in, his icy-blue eyes seeming to glow in realization.

Exhaustion takes over, and I drop to the ground. Each breath requires more effort as I stare up into the bright blue sky. The edges of my vision start to fade into black, and the feminine voice whispers in my mind again, but all I can make out is, "Free me."

Before unconsciousness pulls me under, I watch darkness explode through the battlefield like a bomb. Consuming the land and the sky. I smile when I hear my name roared in the distance. It sounds guttural and demonic; I can't help but feel comforted by the sound. A villain's love is dark, obsessive, and selfish. It is all consuming and will dig its claws into you so deeply you will never be able to escape. The king made a grave error in taking the only thing keeping him sane. That kept him from destroying the kingdoms completely. Me.

I'm drowning in the darkness when a searing pain drags me from the recesses of my mind. I can't stop the grunt I release when I feel hands apply pressure to my wound. I can vaguely hear yelling in the background, but my brain is filled with too much fog to make out the voices. My eyes flutter open to find Kas standing above me, his face streaked with blood. I look briefly at his hands covering my wound, then groan. "That's a lot of blood."

Kas's dark hazel eyes snap up to mine, and for the first time since meeting him, I see devastation and fear in his gaze. His eyes flick back to my abdomen, and he stutters as he says, "I-I can't stop it. I'm sorry… I'm so sorry, Princess."

The nickname sounds like a prayer on his lips. I smile as I try to console him, "It's okay, shh, it's okay. Just breathe. You don't have to be sorry for anything, Grumpy Man. I've got you, and you've got me."

"I can't make it stop," he chokes out.

I can feel the talons of darkness taking hold. Wanting to drag me away from my men. I try to fight it, to hold on. I need to make sure everyone is okay. My voice is weak as I try to reassure him. "Shh… it's okay."

He must hear the exhaustion in my voice because his turns panicked, "Don't close your eyes!"

I force my eyes open again and find him staring at me. "I was just resting them," I say with a sigh.

I hear another voice yell, "The healers are on their way!"

Kas's eyes never leave mine as he nods. "Keep your eyes on me, Princess."

Breathing is getting difficult, and I can feel each stuttered beat of my heart. My voice is weak as I ask, "Where's Dax?"

His eyes flick out to the distance before landing back on me. "He's… busy."

I laugh weakly, then groan. "He's killing everyone in sight, isn't he?"

"Don't worry about him. Worry about yourself."

My hand lazily lifts to rest against his cheek. I'm leaving streaks of blood behind as I caress his cheek, but he doesn't seem to mind. "I'm not worried… you're with me…"

My eyes fall closed; it's getting too hard to hold them open. I feel a shift in my midsection and then a hand holding mine. I fight to open my eyes again and see Kas has shuffled closer, so he can hold my hand tightly against his cheek.

"Stay with me, Princess. Please... please stay with me. The healers are almost here. Just hang on a little longer," he pleads.

His eyes are consumed by black but almost appear to shimmer like black diamonds. "I'm trying," I whisper. When his eyes squeeze shut, I notice streaks running through the blood on his face. As if being wiped away. My heart stutters, and I know... I know I have to say something in case this is my end. He will never accept an 'I love you' from me because that's not how he shows he loves me. I lick my dry lips and whisper, "I h-hate you, K-kasim. W-with every b-beat of my h-heart."

He lets out a mournful cry as his eyes open again. He knows. He knows our 'I hate yous' have turned to 'I love yous'. We can never give up the 'hate yous' because it's our thing. But the tone of them changed over time. Changed from hostility as we said it with venom, to affection with smiles. He will always be my grumpy man, and I will forever be his princess.

I watch the blood smear across his face as he sucks in a breath. "I-I hate you, too, Princess. So much. It hurts how much I hate you. So don't leave me. Don't leave me, Princess."

I know even if I were to leave, Dax would come find me. He promised he would rip the very fabric between life and death if anything were to happen to me. He will come for me. My vision blurs, and my breathing grows labored. When it clears again, I look up at several figures standing around me; one who stands out from the others.

Swirls of darkness weave around him as he kneels next to my head. He cocks his head as his inky eyes take me in. "Are you trying to fly away from me, Little Raven?" he asks, his voice hoarse.

It takes a bit of effort, but I manage a weak smile. "You better capture me before I get too far."

He shifts, and I feel a hand rest against my chest. "Your soul is mine for reaping. You will forever be tied to me... to us. A raven forever trapped."

I take in the blurry faces surrounding me, and I find it hard to understand now that I fought this connection. My eyes land on Dax, and I say, "I l-love you." Then my eyes shift to take in all of my men, till finally they land on Kas again. I suck in a breath as I force out the words, "I love you all."

My eyes drift closed, and I sigh. I know Dax will catch me before I fly too far. His hand warms before it turns into a burning pain. I scream when my flesh starts to feel as if it's being seared away, but I'm too weak to escape it. All I can feel is pain. PAIN. *PAIN.* Then... nothing.

The cold embrace of darkness is all that greets me. I feel the sensation of fingers caressing me before they grasp me. It feels as if they are holding on so tight. Too afraid to let me go. My men. My men are holding onto my soul. Onto me.

I smile as I finally let the darkness take hold. To consume my every cell because I know I'll be safe. I'll always be safe with my villains. A villain's love is obsessive, and they are too selfish to let me go.

The souls that tether you in life shall hold you captive in death until your return.

Forever bound until death himself severs the tether.

CHAPTER THIRTY

DAX

On the battlefield...

I have never felt such paralyzing fear as I do in this very moment. The strings of fate guide my eyes to meet Eira's, and I see specs of blood marring her lips. Three thoughts rush through my mind in this moment...

1. Why is she by herself?

2. Why is she bleeding?

3. Fate would not be so cruel to take her away from me... would it?

My vision shifts without much thought. Colors become brighter, and my vision grows sharper. I've never minded the enhanced eyesight that comes when my eyes turn black, but right now, I can feel it for the curse that it is. It's as if the battle around me blurs in slow motion, and I can hear each stuttered breath that leaves my gaping mouth. My eyes track Eira as she crumples to the ground.

The world changes fast as it speeds up again. The cold, dead thing inside my chest shatters. My body aches as her name erupts from me, sounding guttural. "Eira!" The world explodes as the darkness within me surrounds the battlefield.

No one sees me coming, and I don't see the bodies in front of me as I slash and cut my way to her side. Friend or foe; it doesn't matter to me. All that matters is getting to Eira. My raven.

I don't know where my brothers are, but I don't care. Eira is the only thing filling my thoughts. She is my obsession. It takes what feels like centuries to make it to her side. Kasim is hunched over her as he tries to staunch the bleeding in her stomach.

I startle when I see his face, his dark hazel eyes shifting to black with his grief. I've never seen my brother-in-arms weep, but the trails of blood smeared down his face tell another story. His eyes shine as he looks back to Eira.

His voice breaks when he says quietly, "It won't stop." He sucks in a breath as he continues, "She's going to die if the bleeding doesn't stop."

Her eyes shift to me as I kneel near her head. Her eyes are glazed over with exhaustion and pain when she smiles softly up at me. My voice is hoarse as I ask, "Are you trying to fly away from me, Little Raven?"

Her smile widens as she whispers, "Capture me before I get too far."

This woman... I can hardly breathe as I watch her eyelids flutter closed before opening again. Have I not suffered enough in my life? Does fate find me so distasteful that I'll be forced to watch the woman I love die in front of me? Must I do the unthinkable and curse her the same way my brothers and I have been? The light in her eyes fades quickly as I shift my body and rest my hand against her chest. "Your soul is mine for reaping. You will forever be tied to me... to us. A raven forever trapped."

She looks around before her eyes land back on mine. Her voice is filled with exhaustion when she says, "I l-love you." I have to bite my lip to hold back the tears that threaten my eyes. It's as if she is saying goodbye.

Her eyes move to the others again before landing on Kasim as she repeats the words. I watch as my brother crumbles under her words. Sobs erupt from him, and I can no longer stop tears of my own from flowing down my face. He holds her hand so tightly to his cheek as his chest heaves in anguish.

I know I need to start the spell, or it will be too late. So, I begin chanting the words as my hand heats against her skin. The scream she releases nearly makes me recoil, but I muscle through the need to pull back. The spell is painful, which is why each of us has a scar on our chest.

The moment her screams cut off, I know her heart does too. I throw the magic of the spell into her chest as I yell, "Pay the price!"

Without hesitation each of my brothers slices their hand, placing their bleeding palm on Eira. Once the spell is complete, I scream for the healers. There is only a short window between finishing the spell and forcing her heart to beat again, or it won't work.

I watch as three healers surround her, pouring their magic into her. There's a snap inside my chest, and I know the magic has taken hold. I can feel her restless soul as it tries to leave this plane of existence. I wrap my spiritual fingers around the orb and hold on tight.

I can feel her writhing and fighting my grasp, but that makes me only hold her tighter. Her emotions wash over me, and I almost release her. Fear's icy fingers try to take hold alongside the pain. She feels unimaginable pain. How was she able to stay so calm in Kasim's arms?

I suck in a breath as I hold her soul closer. My tears fall in earnest as I say softly, "I've got you, Little Raven. You are safe." The orb quivers before settling against me. The cold orb slowly turning warm as I curl myself around her. "I've captured you," I choke out.

Chapter Thirty-One

EIRA

I suck in a breath and immediately regret it when I sit up coughing. Shit, my throat is dry. *Ugh, did I die? Is this death?* Opening my eyes, all I see is darkness. Complete darkness. "Hello?" My voice sounds scratchy as if it hasn't been used in a while.

When a hand suddenly appears out of the dark, I jump with a scream. Pressing a hand to my chest, I try to calm myself when I see it's Ash. "Shit! Ash, you scared me. You're not supposed to be spooky, spooky! That's Rev's job."

As if summoning the shadow himself, he steps out of the darkness, making me squeak. "You men are going to kill me with fright." Okay, maybe... *too soon.*

"NO!" Kasim roars from what I assume is the corner of the room.

I cover my ears from the echo of his roar. "Sorry! Sorry! Can someone at least turn the light on, so I'm not frightened every time one of you pops up out of the dark?"

The lights blare overhead, and I squeeze my eyes closed against the brightness. "Regrets were made," I whine as try to squint through the light in search of the guys. Six figures are cocooned in black swirls of darkness. Well that explains why I couldn't see them in the room when the lights were off.

I look down to find that I'm covered in dried blood. There is *way* more blood covering me than my injury should have allowed. "Uhm... so... blood." Well, that was eloquent.

"Would you like a shower, Snow Bunny?" Asher's voice sounds deeper than normal, and I look up to find his eyes consumed in darkness while wisps of black shadows dance across his body.

Oddly the blood doesn't bother me, it's the fact that my men are surrounded by darkness. "Um... no. I'm good. I would like an explanation for the extra blood, though."

Six hands materialize in front of me, each with a cut running down the center of their palm. "We paid death's price," Ash says from beside me.

My brows furrow until I remember the words from a spell I had read about. I vaguely remember hearing them before I... well, died. I... died. My eyes water as I take in each of my men. My broken villains. Ash's dark shadows disappear as he takes a seat on the bed beside me.

He grasps my hand, and his eyes flicker to their beautiful blue. "Don't... don't cry, Snow Bunny."

I choke on my words as I say, "I'm sorry."

He shakes his head, scooting closer and lifting a hand to my cheek. His eyes glisten as he whispers, "Don't cry... please."

I suck in a breath, trying to keep my tears from falling, but I fail when I see the others move closer. I can't hold back the sob that breaks through, and the darkness surrounding the others disappears as they converge on the bed.

Kasim takes my other hand into his and brings it up to rest on his cheek. He nuzzles his face into my palm as his eyes close. "Don't cry. Please don't cry, Princess."

Rev and Alair take up spots behind Kas to rub up and down one of my legs while Bene and Mir mirror them on the other side.

My vision blurs, the tears refusing to stop. "I'm sorry... so... so sorry. I never meant to leave you all."

Ash's thumb brushes my cheek. "Shh. Shh. Don't—" His voice breaks, and he clears his throat and continues, "Snow bunny, breathe. Breathe for me."

I tug on Ash and Kas to pull them into a hug. Their heads rest on my shoulders as I chant, "I love you. I love you. I love you." I have to say it because the cuts on their palms *prove* how far they are willing to go for me. How much they love me. I wouldn't be here if they didn't.

Ash and Kas each wrap an arm around me and hold me while I sob. Minutes pass as I try to calm myself. Eventually, they both pull back from the hug, and Kas cups my face in his palms. His thumbs caress my wet cheeks as he frowns.

"No more of that. No more tears, Princess. Ugly crying doesn't suit you."

A laugh bubbles out of me as he continues to wipe away my tears. There's a tilt to his lips when his dark hazel eyes meet mine. I smile through the tears and say, "You're so nice to point that out. Thank you."

His eyes flick over my face before they soften. "There she is," he whispers. There's a shine to them as they meet mine. "Missed you..."

I surge forward, pressing my lips to his as I slip my fingers into his long hair. It takes a moment for his lips start to moving against mine. The kiss is slow and soft. Something I didn't expect from him.

His hand slides into my hair, using it to hold me close when I try to pull away. My lips brush against his, and I say, "Hate you, Grumpy Man."

"Hate you more, Princess," he replies.

Humming, I pull away with a smile. "As much as I would *love* to fight you on that..." I peer down at myself before looking at the others. "I may need to take a shower. This blood is beginning to itch."

"Having her clean may help with Dax as well," Bene mutters behind Ash.

Mir smacks him. "Not now, idiot."

Arching a brow, I look at my men. "What's wrong with Dax?"

Rev sighs as he taps on Kas's shoulder and says, "I'll take her to the shower."

Crossing my arms, I narrow my eyes. "I'm not going anywhere until you tell me what is wrong with Dax!"

They share a look before Alair gives in with a sigh and explains, "He did not handle your death well. He knows that you are alive but seeing you that way..." He shakes his head.

My eyes widen. "What's wrong?"

"We held onto your soul while the healers tried to bring you back. They exhausted almost all their magic before your heart started beating again," Bene answers.

Kas's eyes bleed to black as he mutters, "We could feel each time your soul tried to slip away. Dax took the brunt of the spell since he was the one who cast it. He *felt* your soul, Princess. Everything you felt, he felt."

"Everything?" I whisper.

He nods, and I try to jump from the bed. "Then I need to go to him, now!"

Rev catches me the moment I start to fall from getting up too quickly. My brain feels fuzzy and spins from the abrupt movement. "Slow down, Sunshine. Let's get you clean first, so he doesn't think you're a ghost coming to haunt him."

He swings me up into his arms, and I sigh in defeat. "I suppose you're right. This blood is very uncomfortable."

He hums as he begins walking to the bathroom. "Then, let's get you clean." He looks over his shoulder and asks, "Can someone help? I don't think she will be able to stand on her own."

Looking over his shoulder, I find Mir and Bene follow while Alair, Kas, and Ash get to work stripping my bed. I hope they burn that bedspread.

I managed to make it down the hall to Dax's bedroom without much help. I almost tripped a few times, but the others were close behind to catch me. Taking a deep breath, I knock and wait.

There's no answer, so I try the doorknob only to find no resistance. Pulling it open, I'm greeted with total darkness. My hands shake with nervous energy when I take a step into his room. I'm bombarded by a whirlwind of black, swirling and whipping my hair around.

"This isn't safe, Princess," Kas says worriedly from the doorway.

I look over at him with a smile. "I would do it for you. I am the calm within the storm, am I not?"

"Yes," he relents reluctantly.

I give him a nod before turning back to the room. Taking a deep breath, I step deeper into the heart of the storm as I'm consumed by the black abyss. I walk slowly, trying to feel where I am going with my feet, considering I'm completely blind.

"Dax? Dax, where are you?" I yell into the deafening wind.

The wind suddenly stops, and I freeze. I look around wildly in search of Dax. I can hear each breath he takes in the deafening silence.

His voice echoes around the room as he calls, "Little Raven?"

It's filled with so much pain and devastation. "Yes, Dax." I keep looking around to see if the dark will recede now that he knows I'm here. "Your little raven is here. Come back to me."

The shadows eventually start to dissipate, and in their place stands Dax. He's looking in my direction, his inky eyes filled with so much torment as they flicker between his bright blue irises, then back to black. He's shivering as the wisps of darkness continue to crawl across his body. His voice breaks when he says, "Don't leave me... please... stay..."

I nod and take a step closer. "Of course. I'm here, Dax. I'm not going anywhere."

He waits until I am only a breath away from him before he asks, "Are you real this time, Little Raven?"

I look up at him in confusion. "Of course, I'm real."

His body trembles as he sucks in a breath. "Every time I try to catch you, you slip through my fingers. You're suddenly just gone, leaving only feathers behind."

My eyes sting as I see the fear in his eyes. The fear that if he touches me, he may find I'm only an illusion. I reach up and rest my hand on his cheek. "Your raven hasn't left you."

It takes him a few moments to realize I am touching him. But when he does, he instantly wraps me up in a tight hug. He buries his face in my neck and releases an anguished cry.

He's holding me so tightly; I fear he may suffocate me. It's in this moment that I know his obsidian heart has shattered into thousands of pieces. When I was lying dead on battlefield, there was no hope for his dying heart.

I wrap my arms around him, holding him as tightly as my weak muscles allow. His body continues to shake as he mutters, "My raven. My raven."

My own tears spill over as I reply, "Your raven is safe. I'm safe, and I'm here with you."

He pulls back to look into my eyes. When they meet, I see his are no longer black but a brilliant sky blue. His eyes flick between mine as words rush out of him. "I love you, Little Raven. If you need to hear those words, I will say them as many times as you want. I will say them as much as you need. Just don't leave me again."

I lean forward to softly brush my lips against his. Pulling back, I reply, "I don't need words; I already know." I don't want an 'I love you' from Dax anyway. I want to hear the same words he said when he first confessed his feelings for me. That I am his obsession. That's all I ever want to be.

He presses his lips to mine urgently. Stroking his lips against mine before pulling back. "I need them," he says breathlessly. "I need them, Little Raven."

"I love you, Dax."

CHAPTER
THIRTY-TWO

I come awake with a groan. *Why am I so hot? Ugh, my body feels like shit.* My eyes open slowly and then widen when I meet my reflection. With a frown, I tilt my head to look at the ceiling. *Is that... is that a mirror on the ceiling?* I never noticed that before, but I've also never been inside Dax's chambers before. Did he remove the covering since his father is dead? I notice then that I am being snuggled fiercely by three males.

Dax is cuddled as close to me as possible on my right side, his face smushed into my neck as he breathes softly. Rev is on my left side, mirroring Dax exactly. Kas found a way to lie between my legs with his arms wrapped around my waist and his head resting on my lower abdomen.

The others are sporadically sprawled across the bed. Each sleeping peacefully as I stare up at the ceiling. *Why would Dax put a mirror on the ceiling? Was this the king's old chambers? Well, that thought sours my mood. I do not want to be lying on a bed the king used to lay on. I hope Dax bought a new bed when he moved in here.* Kas adjusts his hold on me, snuggling deeper into my abdomen. Unfortunately, he snuggles right into my bladder, which sends a blaring alarm through my brain.

Shit! I need to pee! I contort my body, trying to wiggle out from between Rev and Dax. Except, it does not go as planned. Instead of freeing myself from them, they both move even closer. Which makes my need to pee so much worse.

"Guys," I say softly, hoping it will only wake the guys closest to me. Rev lets out a snort as he snuggles.

Biting my lip and trying to force EVERY muscle in my body to keep my bladder from erupting, I say a bit louder, "Guys."

Mir mumbles something, but he doesn't move. I'm about to burst! "Guys!" I finally yell.

Every. Single. One of them jumps off the bed, arms outstretched and ready to fight off an attacker. I don't even care as I jump up from the bed and yell, "OH, THANK THE GODDESS!" I run as fast as I can to the bathroom, hoping my bladder holds.

I hear Kas yell behind me, but there is no stopping me. "Eira!"

"I need to pee!" I screech, barely managing to sit down in time before the floodgates open. I'm hunched over, which may be an odd position, but the relief I feel from emptying my bladder is amazing.

There's a knock on the doorframe, but I don't move. "Little Raven?"

I'd forgotten to close the door in my haste. I wave a dismissive hand in the air. "I'm okay. My bladder would have ruptured if I had waited any longer, though. Kasim was using it as a pillow."

"Are you sure?"

I hum as I finish washing my hands. "It would have been pretty embarrassing if I had wet the bed," I call with a laugh.

"Forgive us for entrapping you, Little Raven."

His voice gives me pause as I meet my reflection in the mirror. My eyes widen when I find all seven of my men standing awkwardly by the door. Turning the sink off, I arch a brow in question. "I didn't mind the cuddling, Dax."

He gives me a nod but doesn't meet my eyes. I look down to find that I'm covered. I'm not naked, although that would normally make him stare, not look away. *So why won't he meet my eyes?* My gaze travels over each of my men, and I find that none of them will make eye contact. My panic begins to build, thinking I've done something wrong. I don't even realize it until Asher is gripping my face, saying softly, "Calm yourself, Snow Bunny. Your eyes turned black, and you are creating swirls of darkness."

My eyes widen as I see the reflection of my eyes within his. They are completely engulfed in black, and I notice the swirls caressing his bare skin. "Ash," I start as I try to gulp down air in my panicked state.

He gently caresses my cheeks, and I raise my hands to grip his wrists. He presses his forehead against mine and says, "Breathe. Breathe with me, Snow Bunny."

I work to match his breathing as he takes slow, deep breaths. When my panic starts to fade, and I'm breathing normally again, I see the black smoke disappear. He pulls away with a smile as he looks down at me. "There she is. I didn't realize how odd it would be to see you without your mahogany eyes."

"Yes, well, I had that seven times over," I reply with a huffed laugh.

Bene comes to stand beside me and rubs a hand up and down my back. "What caused you to panic like that, My Dragoness?"

Finding it silly now, I duck my eyes as I feel my cheeks flush. "It's stupid now that I think about it."

Bene's brows furrow as he says, "Nonsense."

Mir comes to stand on my other side. "What caused you to panic, Darling?"

"I thought I had done something wrong," I mumble.

"What makes you think you did something wrong?" Alair asks from his spot behind Bene.

My men close in around me as I shrug. "None of you would meet my eyes. I thought I had done something to upset you."

Their eyes widen as they exchange looks with each other. Rev huffs out a sigh, then says, "Nothing you do will cause us upset, Sunshine."

"We are upset with ourselves, Princess, not you," Kas admits.

I look between my men until my eyes meet Dax's. "You are upset with yourselves?"

Dax nods and shifts his gaze downward, so it no longer meets mine. I lightly push between the others to make my way over to him. Reaching my hand up to rest against the center of his chest, I feel his rapid heartbeat as he stiffens under my touch. "Why are you upset, love?" I ask in a whisper.

He answers quietly, "We are true villains, Eira. We could not protect you. We failed you."

With my other hand, I grab his to place his palm over my steady heart. Each beat is a testament to how they saved me. How *he* saved me. "Do you feel that?" He nods and I continue, "My heart beats *because* of all of you. It beats because you cast the spell and were willing to pay the price."

His voice breaks when he says, "We have cursed you."

I move the hand I have pressed against his chest to cup his cheek and shift his face, so his glassy blue eyes meet mine. With a gentle smile, I say, "You hold a piece of me within yourself now. All of you hold a piece of me forever. If that is what it means to be cursed, then so be it."

His free hand comes up to rest on my cheek as his eyes shift to black, giving away how much this upsets him. "This is not what I wished for you."

Not liking the pain I hear in his voice, I release my hold on his cheek and back away. His eyes widen for a moment as if he thinks I'm rejecting him until he sees the big smile on my face. "What are you doing, Little Raven?"

I begin stripping off my clothes, leaving myself completely bare in front of my men. I was planning to take a shower anyway. My vision shifts, and I realize my eyes must be black now. I notice that colors are sharper and more pronounced, as if I'm a predator in search of prey.

"I am yours," I state with conviction before my eyes shift to each of my men. "I am all of yours." Making my way over to the shower, I peek over my shoulder at them with a smirk. "If I am to be cursed forever, then show me just how cursed I am. Show me how wicked the villains I have bound to my soul to are."

Without hesitation, Mir strips off his clothes and slowly stalks over to me. "You want to know how wicked we can be?"

I hum as he stands naked in front of me. Lightly trailing a finger down his chest, I reply, "Your darkness does not scare me, Mir." My fingers caress the metal balls around the head of his cock before wrapping tightly around it and giving him a slow stroke. He sucks in a breath as I release him. Sliding my fingers around his balls, I give them a soft squeeze. Before I release them, I feel the cool bite of metal on my fingertips. I grin as I slide my finger to the spot between his balls and ass to find a small metal hoop. Seems I've found his secret piercing. I press the area before allowing my nail to hook in the loop and give it a tug.

His eyes instantly turn black, and he growls, "Do not tease me, Darling."

"Who's teasing?"

He snarls and slides his hands down over my ass to lift me up. He nips at my breasts, making me groan. "Are you sure you want my darkness?" Mir asks.

I suck in a breath when I feel his dark tendrils caress my skin. "Yes," I say with a breathy sigh. I look over to see the others are still staring at me, their eyes full of hunger. The looks they send me have me clenching my thighs together, desperate for friction where I need it the most.

When I meet Kas's gaze, I know exactly what to say to make him lose his tightly wound control. I groan when Mir sucks on my nipple. "Kas," I whine.

He grunts. "What do you want, Princess?"

Moaning, I slip my fingers into Mir's hair to pull him deeper into my chest, loving how he sucks and nips my breasts. "Fuck me like you hate me," I say breathlessly.

Dark tendrils fill the room as Kas rips off his clothes and marches over to us. Mir has me pressed against the shower wall until Kas steps into it with us. "Move," Kas demands.

Mir chuckles against my breast and pulls me away from the wall. "You've done it now, Darling."

I scream when two fingers roughly slam into my cunt. It melts into a moan as Kas places a soft kiss on my shoulder before nipping it. "Do you want my cock, Princess?"

"Yes," I whine as he continues at a slow but forceful pace with his fingers. It's not enough, though; I want more. I need more.

He nips my shoulder, and with a growl, he demands, "Then you better come. You don't get my fat cock until you soak my fingers."

"Need more," I cry out as I try to force his fingers deeper. But no matter how much I try, I can't get him deeper. Mir has me confined as Kas slowly fucks me with his fingers.

"You need more, Princess? Then beg. Beg for another finger in that needy fucking cunt."

"Please, Kas. I need another finger. I need more of you."

Mir hums and says, "Now, I know you can beg better than that."

My eyes burn as I choke on a sob of need. The heat in my abdomen keeps building but refuses to push me over the edge. "Please!" I beg. "Please, Kasim. I need more. I need another finger. I need you to fuck my needy cunt with your fingers till I see stars. Please."

Mir chuckles and licks the tears that are rolling down my cheeks. "You beg so well, Darling."

When Kas's fingers slide out, he inserts another finger, and my head falls back onto his shoulder. I'm panting as he quickens his pace. "Yes. Yes, Kasim! Fuck me like you hate me!"

His other hand slides in between me and Mir to tease my clit. I whimper when the pleasure builds to the point of it being almost painful. "Please, Kasim. Please, I'm so close."

He continues to fuck me with his fingers, then he growls, "Come!" He bites down on my shoulder at the same time as he pinches my clit. His fingers slam into me, hitting just the right spot to make me scream and come undone. I feel myself tighten around his fingers, and he hums in satisfaction.

I whimper as he removes his fingers but groan when he replaces them with his cock, forcing himself deep into my tight channel. I bite my lip as his thrusts turn just as forceful as the fingers he used to fucked me.

Mir holds my upper body while Kas tightly holds my hips. I have a feeling his grip will leave fingerprint bruises on my hips, but I don't care. The cuts across my skin were Dax's way of claiming me. Finger-prints can be how Kas claims me. I want all of them to claim me in their own way.

"Your tight cunt grips my fucking cock so perfectly, Princess. You were made for me. Made to take my cock so prettily." He pinches my clit again, and I'm surprised by the orgasm he draws from me. "Fuck," he growls. I look over my shoulder to see that he is looking down at where we are joined. His eyes are completely black as he huffs out, "You're creaming all over my cock, Princess. So fucking beautiful."

"Kas," I pant out.

His eyes meet mine, and he groans, "Don't look at me like that. I'm not going to last if you do."

Letting my eyes flutter closed, I rest my forehead against Mir. "Kas," I pant again. "Kasim, I want to kiss you."

He grunts and pulls out of me, but within moments, I'm pulled away from Mir and pushed against the shower wall. He thrusts back inside me as he seals his lips to mine. I groan into his kiss while he devours my mouth with each thrust. He kisses just like he fucks. Hard and hungry. Like a starving man who believes my mouth and pussy will satiate his hunger.

I push him away to gasp for breath. He rests his forehead against mine as we both pant, trying to catch our breath. I whisper, "I love you, Kasim."

He lets out a sound similar to a keen as he pounds into me. "Fuck."

I lift my hands to tangle my fingers in his hair as I briefly press my lips to his, whispering, "Fuck me like you love me."

His hips stutter, and his eyes close. Kas thrusts slow, turning gentle and languid as his eyes open to meet mine. They are no longer black but dark hazel. He brushes his lips against mine and whispers back, "I do. So much, Princess."

For some reason, a moment between the two of us months ago flashes through my mind. When he had asked who would lose me. Who would mourn me? I don't want to ruin this moment, but I can't stop myself. I pull away just enough that my eyes meet his, and I ask in a hushed voice, "Would you mourn me, Kas?" When he pauses mid-thrust, and his eyes widen, it is clear he remembers that moment.

I watch as his eyes turn glassy, and he reaches up with one hand to caress my cheek. "I would not be able to mourn you, Princess. To mourn another, they first must have a heart."

He moves his hips in slow thrusts, his eyes never leaving mine as he waits for my response. I'm not sure how to respond as I can only say his name. "Kasim?"

He lowers his lips to meet mine, lovingly brushing a soft kiss to them that makes my eyes burn. He rests his forehead rests mine as he continues to thrust, not pausing as he says, "My heart would cease to beat. I would have no heart left to mourn you with. My soul would follow yours without question."

He repeatedly hits just the right spot inside of me, and my pleasure grows. My eyes burn, and I can see the love he feels for me in his as he stares back at me. "Kas," I quietly choke out.

He kisses me softly. "There won't be a moment to mourn you because I will never be without you long enough to do so."

I cry out when my orgasm hits, making him growl, and his thrusts begin to quicken. "You. Are. Mine," he grunts out.

My fingers tighten in his hair as I say, "I am yours."

"My Princess." He growls as he slams into me.

I manage to open my eyes just enough to meet his, and I reply, "You are mine. My Grumpy Man."

With a roar, he slams into me one last time, and I feel the warmth of his seed fill me. He pants as he rests his forehead on my shoulder. His words are only loud enough for me to hear when he replies, "You can call me whatever you wish, so long as I am yours. Forever yours, Princess."

Chapter Thirty-Three

Dax is still acting weird even after our sexy session in the shower. Huffing out a sigh, I finally blurt out, "Dax, what's wrong?"

We are currently huddled up in my room. Which is nice, considering the mirror on his bedroom ceiling freaked me out a bit. Maybe I should ask about the mirror? Though that might be a random question to ask right now. Hum… question for another time, I suppose. My men are sporadically situated around the room; Ash and Kas are on the bed with me, while the others have pulled up chairs to sit around the bed. I think it may be time for a bigger bed soon, so all of us can lie in here together.

He rubs the back of his head, still avoiding my gaze. "I found a spell in one of the books in the library. I'm not sure if it will work, which is why I'm a bit hesitant to say anything."

"I can tell that whatever it is weighs heavily on your mind. Just talk to me, Dax."

He rubs a hand down his face and stands from his chair. He begins pacing in front of the bed and sputters out, "I found a spell that will allow you to speak to the dead. It will only work for a limited amount of time, though." His eyes meet mine, and I realize why he searched for this spell.

I sit up and crawl to the end of the bed as I ask, "You wanted a spell in case I didn't make it?"

He nods sharply as he continues to pace. "I know you were very close with your parents. That your father was lost at sea, and my father killed your mother." He winces at that last part.

I frown, trying to understand why he would mention this now. Then it clicks, and my eyes widen as I jump up from the bed. "I can speak to them?"

He winces at my shout but says, "You can speak to only one. The spell is limited, and it requires a lot of magic, so you will not be able to speak to them again for a while."

Who should I talk to? I can only choose one. One moment with a parent again. I bite my lip. "My mother. I wish to speak to my mother."

"Are you sure, Little Raven? This may not work. I've never done a spell like this before."

I nod as I tighten my robe. "Yes. I want to see my mother."

He watches me for a moment before nodding. "Okay. I'll need some space." He points at the chairs and says, "I'll need this area cleared." Pulling out a knife, he pricks his finger and kneels.

"Dax?"

He looks up at me with a soft smile. "This spell requires payment. Blood is all that is needed. Nothing more, I promise."

I nod as I back away, giving him enough room to draw symbols on the floor. It's a few moments later when he nods and looks back up at me. "I'll need a strand of your hair."

Running my hands through my hair, a few strands come loose. I'm careful of the symbols as I make my way over to him. Handing the strands over, he smiles and points to the edge of the circle. "You will need to stand there."

I do as I'm told, moving over to the edge of the circle. Once I'm where he wants me, he begins to chant in another language, and the symbols start to give off a red glow. He places the strands of hair in the blood by his fingers as he ends the chant.

I wait on bated breath, then there's a sharp crack and a flare of light. I squeeze my eyes shut against the onslaught of light. I blink open my eyes when it seems to have faded. I can't help but gasp as a ghostly image of my mother stands in front of me. I can see Dax's wide eyes through her body. I dare not breathe as I wait to see if this is real.

She looks around for a moment before her eyes land on me. They widen, and her voice comes through muffled. It's almost too muted for me to catch. "Eira?"

My hands fly up to cover the sob that rips from my throat as my vision blurs. "Mom?"

She smiles softly and says, "My Little Snowflake. You have grown so much."

I can't stop the words as they fly out of my mouth, "I'm sorry, Mommy! I'm so sorry that I killed you! I'm so sorry! I couldn't stop him! I'm sorry! I'm sorry!"

Her eyes hold a ghostly shimmer as she says, "Oh, my darling. It wasn't your fault. I should have taken your counsel more seriously."

I shake my head as tears stream down my face. "I'm sorry."

She reaches out as if to touch me but then realizes she's not actually here. "Enough of that, Eira. You have grown so much. A beautiful woman. We only have so long to speak, I imagine."

My eyes flick to Dax, and I see tears streaming down his face as he watches me. I realize that my connection with him is the strongest. He can feel everything I'm feeling in this moment. I try to bottle everything up and pack it away.

He grunts as he shakes his head. "Do not hide from me, Little Raven."

"But..."

His shimmering blue eyes harden as he says, "It is well worth the pain for you to have this moment with your mother. Do not waste it, Little Raven."

Taking a deep breath, I blurt as much out as I can in the short time we have together. "I was tortured by the king for many years, but it made me strong. These men..." I gesture to the guys around me. "These men saved me from him. The rules of the world have changed, and even though they may be villains... I love them. I love them very much."

She looks at the men around me with a soft smile. "As long as they love you, Little Snowflake. That is all I wish for you."

Her image begins to shimmer, and my tears renew. "Is Daddy there?"

She nods. "He is."

"I died for a moment, but these men brought me back," I choke out. "I wanted to be with you and Daddy so much, but I couldn't leave them behind."

She smiles as her image wavers again. "I'm glad you stayed behind."

I rub my eyes, trying to wipe away the tears, not wanting to miss a single moment with my mom. "Tell Daddy I love him! Tell him I found seven amazing men who love and take care of me. Tell him that he would approve."

She shimmers again. "I will baby."

"I can only hold her here for a few more minutes," Dax says, grunting with exertion. I look over to find his face soaked with tears as he watches me. He can feel how happy I am to have this moment, but also the heartbreak of losing my mother all over again.

"I miss you!" I sob.

"I miss you, too, baby," she says as her image wavers again.

"I killed him, Mom. I killed the king, and we took back our kingdom. I'll make you and Daddy proud! I'll be the best queen I can be."

"Oh, my Little Snowflake. Your dad and I have always been proud of you." Her image wavers again until there's barely a whisper of her image.

"Mommy!" I sob.

She gives me a wide smile. "We are so proud of you. Always remember that. We love you, Little Snowflake."

I fall to my knees as her image disappears. I wrap my arms around my middle as I bend over sobbing, my forehead resting against the cool floor. Arms engulf me, and I'm lifted. Dax wraps me in his arms, holding me tight.

"I've got you. I've got you, Little Raven." His voice comes out choked as he holds me close.

"Dax," I whimper.

He gently rocks me, then softly says, "Break if you must. Break but know that I will be right here to pick up every last broken piece of you. Shatter into thousands of shards, it does not matter. I will still be here."

"*We* will be here," Mir says softly, his fingers tangling in my hair.

I can't hold back my sobs any longer as I cry into Dax's chest, mourning everything I've lost. I never had the luxury of mourning my father when I was still needed to help my mother. I couldn't mourn my mother or my only friend while under the watchful gaze of the king. Charlotte had been my one and only friend, and I have missed her company. I mourn the loss of myself, and the woman I had to become. Lastly, I mourn the men my guys could have been if the world we lived in was not so cruel.

CHAPTER THIRTY-FOUR

Breakfast is interrupted when Dax marches through the door and announces, "We need to make our way to Arcelia."

I look around the room to find the others watching me with concern. Brows pinched, I ask, "What?"

Asher is the first to speak up. "Are you well enough to travel?"

I shrug as I continue to eat. "I'm feeling as well as one can after briefly dying."

Kas growls. "Can we not joke about the fact that you died?"

I smirk in his direction. "Are you admitting you like me, Kasim?"

He narrows eyes at me and grumbles, "You know the answer to that, Princess."

Snickering, I hurry to finish my breakfast. I love messing with the grump; he makes it so easy. "So we need to go to Arcelia?"

Dax nods and stands in front of me. "Now that the king is dead, we need to present a united front, so no one tries to take the throne in my absence."

It takes a moment for me to realize what he's saying. We killed the king, which, by default, means Dax is now the king of not only Wylan but Arcelia as well. But I am confused as to why we need to present a united front. "What does presenting a united front have to do with me? You are now the king of not only Wylan but also Arcelia."

He arches a brow. "I am the King of Wylan only. *You* are the rightful Queen of Arcelia. If we wish to ease the nerves of the people of Cybele and Islwyn, we need to show that Arcelia and Wylan are peaceful allies."

Mouth agape, I stutter, "Queen of Arcelia?"

He nods as he pushes away from the counter. "Of course. Why would you not be queen?"

"I just assumed you would want to be the king of both kingdoms."

His brows pinch as he shakes his head. "My father stole your kingdom from you, why would I wish to do the same? It is your kingdom to rule, not mine."

I look around the room, starting to panic as I ask, "Does that mean you no longer wish for me to stay here with you? You wish for me to stay in Arcelia?"

The men converge on me, and Asher wraps his arms around me. He tightens his embrace as he says, "We do not wish to be rid of you, Snow Bunny. You are welcome to stay with us if you wish."

Dax reaches across the table to grasp my hand and says, "I wish only to give you back your kingdom. We can rule together if you would like, Little Raven."

I take a deep breath to calm my panic and nod without hesitation. I am not sure I can rule by myself. I'm still learning the ways of this new world. I don't feel comfortable doing so without my men. Taking a deep breath, I ask, "Is there a reason we must go to the castle today? I would rather wait if possible."

A look of guilt passes over Dax's face before he huffs out a sigh. "We must ensure the spells and curses my father attached to the castle have been dispelled."

Humming, I ask, "If we destroy everything he has spelled, will that turn the kingdoms back to normal?"

Kas snorts a laugh. "Normal? This is normal."

Rolling my eyes, I reply, "You know what I mean. The kingdoms will not be overshadowed by darkness any longer."

Dax grunts and replies, "Actions have very real consequences. My father's actions caused many things to play out. Unfortunately, we must live with the consequences of his decisions."

Arching a brow, I ask, "So... that's a no?"

Dax hums. "We will most likely always live in a world overshadowed by my father's darkness. His influence will forever stain this land. The echoes of the spells he placed will always be there. This isn't a fairytale where the villain dies, and their curse disappears with them."

"Well, that's unfortunate," I say with a groan before continuing, "So we need to make our way to Arcelia today then?"

Dax nods. "It will be best to just get it over with."

Getting to my feet, I ask, "Is there a reason this needs to be done so quickly?"

Dax and his men exchange glances before he looks back to me. "There is one specific item my father had in his grasp. I fear if anyone were to get their hands on it, we may face a far greater evil than my father."

"What item is that?"

"A mirror," he grunts.

My eyes widen as unwelcome memories of the castle covered in mirrors flicker through my brain. The mirrors in the king's possession that melt into silver tentacles. I shiver at the memory. "Will the mirror be dangerous?"

Dax shakes his head as he leaves the kitchen. "It needs a being to connect itself to, in order to hold power."

I nod as I hustle after him. "Then let us make haste to rid our kingdoms of anything that man ever touched."

I can't stop the shiver of unease I feel as we journey to Arcelia. It's odd how this place no longer feels like home; instead, Wylan is where I feel the safest.

Rev had said that the path to Arcelia should be safe, considering the creatures that used to roam under the king's control no longer have magic commanding them. Alair had pointed out that just because the king no longer controls them doesn't mean they aren't dangerous.

"Will they not die, considering the magic that controls them is no longer there?" I ask in curiosity.

Dax looks over to me as he answers, "The magic that controls them is no longer there, yes. But the magic that revived them is still active. Until we destroy the mirror, the death-bringers will still move about the lands."

I nod. "So once we destroy the mirror, its magic will then leave those it has touched?"

Dax shrugs. "That is the hope. I doubt that the effects from the magic will disappear completely, but those controlled by it will hopefully be able to find peace."

"That would be preferable," I say as our horses pull to a stop outside the grand front steps leading to the castle doors.

"Welcome home, Queen Eira," Mir says with a smile.

I look at him briefly, shooting him a small smile, before turning back to the castle. I take in the grand majesty of what was once my home. The place where I was raised and where my family was murdered. "This isn't my home anymore," I whisper.

Bene walks up beside my steed and offers me his hand to help dismount my horse. His smile is gentle as he says, "This is where you called home for so long. How can it no longer be your home? Are you not pleased to be here?"

Once I'm settled on the ground, I rise on my tiptoes to press a soft kiss to his lips. "My home is where my heart is, and my heart belongs with seven males who reside in Wylan."

"Is that so?" he says with a bright smile.

I pull away to look briefly at the others before peering up at the castle again. "This place holds only memories. It no longer holds my heart nor my love."

"Are you saying that we hold not only your heart but your love as well, Princess?" Kas asks.

I can't stop myself from messing with him as I reply, "Everyone except for you, Kas."

His eyes widen before narrowing again when he sees the smirk I'm trying to hide. "Bad Princess."

"The baddest," I reply with a wink. Taking a deep breath, I tangle my fingers with Bene's. "Let's get this over with. I would like to return home as soon as possible."

Dax tangles his fingers with my free hand and lifts it, pressing a kiss to the back of it. With a smile, he says, "As My Queen wishes."

Chapter Thirty-Five

The moment I step through the doors of my old home, my stomach twists. The former king's dark and twisted powers caress my skin. "Why does it feel like I'm walking through molasses?"

Dax looks at me with an arched brow. "What do you mean?"

My eyes roam the halls as we walk. "Do you not feel it? The oppressive feeling of the magic used here?"

Dax shakes his head. "I don't feel anything."

"Maybe, I'm..."

Dax interrupts me before I can finish my thought. "Do not discount your feelings. We will follow your lead. Take us to where you feel the magic is the most powerful."

I freeze at the trust he is putting on me. "You—you believe me?"

His gaze softens as he nods. "Of course. You were the one who killed my father. It's possible his magic attached to you, and it could be that what you are feeling is the residual power he left behind here."

Taking a deep breath, I nod with renewed confidence. The feeling of the dark tendrils of power caressing my skin is less disturbing with my men by my side. "This way."

My hands tighten in Dax and Bene's as we continue through the castle. The magic becomes so thick it's getting harder to breathe. I fight my way through the need to gulp down air as we approach the throne room.

The moment my hand touches the door, I have to suck in a deep breath as the feeling almost overwhelms me. Dax's hand tightens in mine. "Eira?"

Squeezing my eyes shut, I try to breathe through the uncomfortable feeling. "In here," I choke out.

I hear the clang of swords being drawn behind me as Dax releases my hand. "I'll take a quick look around first. Stay here, Little Raven."

I nod and try to focus on taking deep breaths. The last thing I need is to have a panic attack. The moment he opens the door, I'm bombarded with echoing screams. My hands immediately rise to cover my ears, and I let out a scream of my own. Dax's wide eyes meet mine as my vision changes. I know my eyes are engulfed in black as colors around me sharpen, but so do the sounds.

"Make them stop!" I scream as I drop to my knees. Thousands of screaming voices surround me at once. They beg and plead for me to end it all. To free them from their eternal torment. I feel someone shake me, but I pay them no mind as I'm locked in my own eternal hell.

One voice rings out louder than the rest. A feminine voice yells, "Free me!"

"I don't know how!" I scream back.

The voices begin chanting in sync, "Mirror. Mirror. Break. Break."

I try to focus through blurry eyes from the outside of the room. I can't see anything from my vantage point, so I scream, "Mirror! Break the mirror!"

I'm sure only a few moments pass, but it feels like an eternity before everything goes silent again. Taking a deep breath, I chance uncovering my ears and look around. Shattered glass is spread across the room, and I look up to find seven males peering down at me in worry.

Asher is the first to break the silence. "Are you okay, Eira?"

I take a shuddering breath and give him a hesitant nod. "I think so," I whisper.

"What the fuck just happened?!" Kas yells.

I hiss as his loud voice makes my head pound. I hear a thump and look up to find Kas holding his face and Rev giving him a death glare. "Did you not just see her screaming in pain from voices we couldn't hear? I don't believe you yelling will help!"

I chuckle at my dark shadow. "I'm okay, Spooky."

Rev's eyes shift to mine, softening when he says, "I do not like seeing you in pain." Then he smirks. "Unless I am the one causing it."

I shake my head but regret it when my head starts to pound. Pressing my fingers to my temples and wishing this headache would go away, I ask, "Is there anything else we need to destroy while we are here?"

Dax kneels in front of me. "The mirror was the most important thing. We can wait on everything else."

"No, we should get everything done now, so we can return home." I lift my eyes to meet his bright blue ones and say, "I do not wish to return for a while."

He nods in understanding before leaning to press a kiss to my forehead. "I will get it done, Little Raven." He looks to Kasim and Reverie. "The two of you will stay here until we are finished."

They nod and make their way over to my side, taking a seat next to me while the others leave to take care of everything else.

"Are you well?" Kasim asks softly.

He looks properly chastised by Rev, and I can't help but chuckle. "I am well, Grumpy Man."

I look to Rev next. "Can we go outside. I really don't want to be here anymore." He nods and lifts me into his arms. "I am perfectly capable of walking myself, Rev."

He hums but continues to carry me out of the castle anyway. "I know. But I wish to hold you close for a bit. To know you are well."

I keep forgetting that it hasn't been long since I technically died in the battle for the kingdom. I snuggle into him and say, "I do not mind being spoiled for a bit."

He huffs out a laugh, then Kas snorts and says, "I told you; I knew you were a spoiled princess."

With a smirk, I tease, "Do you not like spoiling me, Kasim?"

He grunts. "I did not say that."

Before I can reply, the others march out of the castle. I look over Rev's shoulder. "That was quick."

Dax is in the lead, and he shrugs. "You wished to leave as soon as possible."

I roll my eyes and reply, "We do not need to leave immediately. You could have taken your time."

Asher comes up beside Rev and me and presses a kiss to my cheek. "We would much rather be with you, Snow Bunny."

I snort a laugh. "I know you would rather be with me, but that doesn't mean you have to rush to destroy the items in the castle."

"We didn't rush around the castle destroying things if that is what you are implying," Bene tells me with a smirk.

"The look on your face has me doubting the truth to your words."

He shrugs as Mir asks, "Would you believe it if I were to say the words?"

I shake my head with a laugh. "Nope."

"Shall we return home now that we have finished?" Alair asks from atop the front stairs of the castle.

Dax nods. "Let's head back before it gets dark. We may have destroyed the king's items that held the magic, but we don't know how it will affect the land and its creatures now that he's gone."

I nod in agreement. I know that the death-bringers will still be wandering around, but we don't know if the magic held in the castle allows them free will or if they are still tainted by the magic.

"Let's go home."

Chapter Thirty-Six

I'm mid bite when Dax enters the kitchen. He looks around the room till his eyes land on me. My fork is still in my mouth when he smiles, making his way over to me. I'm frozen, which I'm sure is a vision with my cheeks puffed out with eggs and a fork hanging out of my mouth.

"Good morning, Little Raven." He presses a soft kiss to my forehead before popping a bite of egg into his mouth with his fingers.

Snapping out of my haze, I pull the fork from my mouth as I try to talk around my mouthful. "Why are you in such a good mood this morning?"

"Am I not allowed to be in a good mood, Little Raven?"

I arch a brow as I wave the empty fork in his direction. "You aren't normally this... happy."

He smirks and asks, "Did you forget what today is?"

Brows pinching, I try to think. It's been about a week since we returned from Arcelia. I briefly remember Dax mentioning that we need to join the kingdoms to prevent any uprisings. Wait... wait! My eyes flick to meet his as he smirks at me. His smirk grows when my eyes widen in realization.

"No... it's too early," I whisper.

"It's never too early for a coronation," Ash counters with a chuckle.

"I don't want to leave!" I say in a panic. If I'm crowned Queen of Arcelia, I would have to stay there until the people are under control. But I don't want to part with my men.

The men exchange confused glances, then Rev asks, "Why would you have to leave?"

"We are doing the coronation for Arcelia, correct?"

Dax nods and replies, "Yes. But I am still confused as to why you would have to leave."

"If I am to be crowned Queen of Arcelia, I would have to stay in the kingdom until my rule is accepted. We will be separated for an unknown length of time. I don't want that."

Kas arches a brow. "Do you really think we would force you to go back and stay in that kingdom?"

Feeling confused now, I ask, "Is that not how things are done?"

Mir shakes his head. "That was never the plan."

Dax reaches across the table to clasp my hand. "The coronation today is for you becoming Queen of not only Arcelia, but Wylan as well."

I feel arms wrap around me as a warm chest settles against my back. Mir's voice is soft as he asks, "Do you really think we could part from you now, Darling?"

From beside me, Alair hums and asks, "Do you really think we would risk losing you again?"

Dax's grip on my hand tightens as my eyes meet his. "You are ours, Little Raven. In a cage of our making."

Warmth envelopes me, and I can feel the magic of our bound souls. Their love surrounds me in its obsessive and smothering hold. To others it may feel suffocating, but all I feel is safe and cherished within their cage, not trapped.

I can't stop the smile that splits my face as I say, "Then, I suppose we should hurry this coronation along." I twist my hand in Dax's, so my fingers are tangled with his. "I do hope there's a crown."

He grins. "Only the best for you, My Queen."

I tap Mir's arms as I say, "Well, let's get on with it."

Mir presses a kiss to my neck before releasing his hold on me. Dax doesn't release my hand as he guides me around the table. "We have a dress laid out for you on your bed, as well as shoes." Pressing a kiss to my knuckles, he releases my hand with a bow. "We will wait outside your door once we are ready."

Smiling, I give him a slight bow, then make my way to my bedroom. Though, I haven't used it much in the last few weeks. The guys wanted me as close as possible, which meant we slept in Dax's room.

I open the bedroom door to find the dress Dax mentioned, though, I'm not sure dress is the word I would use to describe it. The only fabric piece of it is the bodice, while the skirt is made up of sheer material and high slits. Next to the dress is a pair of three-inch stilettos. My eyes catch on something in the corner of the room. Looking over, I find a mirror adorned in gold filigree.

Smiling to myself, I quickly strip and make my way over to the dress. Slipping it on, I stare back at my reflection. My breasts are plump as they fill the cups of the bodice. I caress the handprint mark on full display over my right breast.

My mahogany eyes meet in the mirror, and I don't think I've ever seen my eyes as bright as they are now. On bare feet, I rush to the bathroom. Pulling out drawers, I try to find the container of crushed coal I'd seen. It must have belonged to a previous queen or princess.

"Found you!" I snatch the small tin of black powder and rush back to the mirror. Opening the tin, I brush a small amount across my eyelids with my fingertips. My smile is wide as I close the tin and meet my gaze in the mirror once more. My eyes are shadowed, but I look like a dark goddess.

Sliding into the heels, I take one last look at myself before heading to the door. The moment the door swings open, seven pairs of eyes shift to me. My body flushes at the sudden attention. I feel bare beneath their gazes on me. Clearing my throat, I say softly, "I hope this is to your satisfaction."

"Is it not to your satisfaction, Little Raven?"

I caress the edges of the sheer fabric, keeping my voice soft as I reply, "It is a bit revealing for my liking. Especially considering there will be hundreds of eyes on me."

I feel cold wisps wrap around my legs and caress me softly, and I know the moment they solidify that they belong to Mir. I can feel his essence as the shadows wrap around my waist. My eyes shift to his, and his cheeks are pink.

He arches a brow. "Is that better, Darling?"

I moan as I feel his shadows drift over my thighs, coming dangerously close to my folds. "That is going to be distracting."

He smirks. "Then we shall make this coronation short."

Taking a deep breath, I shoot him a smirk. "Maybe we can have some fun after." I begin walking past them, my heels clicking across the floor as I add a tantalizing swing to my hips. I wait until I've passed all of them before looking over my shoulder with a wink. "Just imagine fucking me with only my heels and crown on."

A series of growls follow behind me as the shadows caressing my thighs tighten. Between one breath and the next, I'm in the grand hall by the throne. I look around, confused to find all seven men surrounding me, but Reverie is right next to me.

My eyes widen when I realize what happened. With surprise, I ask, "You can transport yourself through the shadows?"

He shrugs as he steps away with a soft smirk. "I have many talents, Sunshine."

I can't stop an eye roll as I look around the room to find hundreds of people gathered. Wow. I wasn't expecting this many people to be in attendance.

Dax steps up beside me as his voice echoes around us, "Thank you all for gathering here. Today, we are blessed to crown the Queen of not only Wylan, but Arcelia as well." His eyes shift to mine as the shadows around my thighs slide closer to my folds. I bite my lip and try to suppress a groan. His eyes glitter with mirth as he continues speaking to his people. "We will keep this coronation brief."

Extending his hand to me, I slip my palm in his. Tugging on my hand, he brings me closer to the throne. He releases me and turns to grab something behind him. When he turns back around, I gasp at the sight in front of me.

In his hands, rests a breathtaking crown. I stand frozen as he smiles, then lifts the crown and places it gently upon my head. I watch his lips move, but I'm too distracted by his soft caresses. My breath hitches as the tendrils drift past my center.

I catch the last of Dax's words as he says, "As the King of Wylan, I now pronounce you the Queen of both Wylan and Arcelia."

Fire builds in my abdomen as the tendrils slide between my folds, and I moan. My vision shifts, and I know my eyes have turned black. My voice echoes as I command, "Everyone, thank you for coming, but please leave now." A smile creases my face as I add, "Except for my men."

Chapter Thirty-Seven

The room clears out surprisingly fast. I wait until I hear the doors to the grand hall close. The thump of them shutting echoes around the room. Sliding my fingertips up my arms, I slip the sleeves of my dress off and shimmy the bodice down and over my hips to drop to the floor. I'm left in nothing but my crown, heels, and Mir's shadows.

I massage my breasts as Mir's shadows slip between my folds again. I moan as I say, "I love your shadows about as much as I love your cock, Mir."

"Pinch your nipples," he orders with a growl.

Doing as instructed, I pinch my nipples when I feel his shadows slip into my cunt, and another massages my bud. I grow wet as his shadows pump in and out. I bite my lip as need grows, and heat pools between my legs.

"She's dripping," Dax hisses.

I can feel my slick begin to slide down my thighs. "More..." I pant, "I need more."

"Come on my shadows, and you can have whatever you wish."

Warmth surrounds me as a kiss is pressed against my hot skin. "Come on his shadows, Snow Bunny." The kiss on my shoulder turns into a sharp bite as Asher's teeth dig in. I pinch my nipples as Mir's shadows increase in size and pump faster.

I come with a scream and squirt all over the floor. Asher groans as he releases my shoulder and bends me forward. Without hesitation, he slams his dick into my still-fluttering cunt. I come again as he forces himself in to the hilt.

His fingers on my hips tighten as he growls, "Fuck! Squeeze my fucking cock, Snow Bunny." He slides out slowly before slamming back in. The pace he sets is slow and deliberate as he continues his harsh thrusts.

Suddenly, Mir is in front of me. He's pumping his cock as he grins down at me. Pre-cum leaks from the tip as he commands, "Open your mouth for me, Darling."

I do without hesitation, and he slips his tip between my wet lips. The metal from his piercings click against my teeth as he fills my mouth. I hum around him as he tangles his fingers in my hair.

Groaning, he licks his lips and looks down at me. "Your puffy, red lips look mesmerizing wrapped around me."

I hum again as I suck deliberately around his dick before lightly running my teeth along the length of his shaft as he pulls out. He growls before he pushes back in. He begins to match his thrusts to Asher's as they fuck me.

I reach up to play with the piercing behind his balls as I hum again. His fingers tighten in my hair, and his breath stutters. "Careful, Darling. You'll have my cum shooting down your throat if you keep that up."

"My cock better be dripping with your cum if he's shooting down your throat, Snow Bunny." Asher grunts as his fingers begin a maddening rhythm across my clit.

I whine around Mir's cock and press my ass into Asher, wanting him deeper. Ash chuckles, and his pace quickens. I look up at Mir, finding him watching me through half-lidded eyes filled with lust.

"Your pleasure filled eyes are drawing me in," Mir says, panting, as his pace quickens to match Ash's.

My abdomen tightens with a coming orgasm. I tug on his hoop piercing while my other hand massages his balls. His fingers tighten their grip in my hair, and he shouts. Balls drawing up, he shoots his cum down my throat. I greedily suck, ensuring I swallow every drop.

Asher pinches my clit as he slams into me. Mir pulls out of my mouth, and I scream out my pleasure, a mixture of saliva and cum dribbling down my chin. Asher pulls out of my tight channel before slamming back in and coming with a roar.

I don't have time to catch my breath as he pulls out of me, and a mixture of our releases slide down my bare thighs to pool on the wooden floor. Kasim immediately takes Asher's place, slipping his fingers into my tight cunt to scoop out the fluid.

I whimper when his fingers slip free and begin pushing the mixture into my taut ass. He massages, using lube to stretch my unused channel. "I'm going to fuck this ass, Princess." He grunts as he teases the hole with the tip of his cock. "You're going to have our cum filling every hole. We are going to own every part of you. Your belly will be swollen with our releases."

"Yes," I pant as I press myself against him. I'm not going to lie; I've become a needy whore for their cocks.

He chuckles darkly as he presses into my now-lubed channel. "Such a good princess."

My knees shake as he begins to slowly seat himself in my ass. Fingers slip into my hair, and I look up to find Rev in front of me. I reach out to steady myself on his thighs.

I don't wait for him to ask; I just slip my mouth around his thick cock and begin to suck greedily. The metal from his piercings clicks against my teeth as he pushes into my mouth, grunting each time one snags on a tooth, but it seems pleasurable for him as he swells thicker in my mouth. I swirl my tongue around the head of his dick. He hums in satisfaction and begins to move his hips, slowly fucking my face. I moan around his cock as Kasim fully seats himself inside me. He's panting as he waits for my body to adjust to his size.

I'm too worked up, too needy to wait, though. I press my ass back into him with a whimper. He chuckles and gives my ass a slap. I moan when I feel my body start to tighten around him, and my cunt clamps around nothing.

"Slap her ass again, brother," Rev says with a grunt.

Kas gives my ass another harsh slap, and my fingers dig into Rev's thighs as my cunt clamps down on thin air. A gush of fluid runs down my bare thighs as I come. Kasim hums in satisfaction. "Did you just cum all over your thighs and the floor?"

I nod around Rev's cock, and Kas chuckles. "Such a good princess, coming just from a spank on your ass. I wonder how worked up I can get you if I stop moving in your needy ass?" He runs a hand over my ass cheek before giving it a hard smack. "What if I only slap your ass?"

I whimper when Kas freezes, burying himself to the hilt as he runs a finger down my spine. "Suck Rev's cock, Princess."

I'm distracted by the feeling of being stuffed full, but the pleasure of his movements dissipates the longer he stays still. Fingers tighten in my hair, and I look up to meet Rev's coal-black eyes as he growls and says, "Suck my cock as I fuck your face, Sunshine."

Kas delivers another slap, and I do as I'm told. My pleasure builds with each harsh smack. Tears are streaming down my face as Rev fucks my mouth, and the need for release continues to build with no relief. My fingers dig into Rev's thighs as I hum around his cock. His thrusts stutter, and he groans. His cum coats my mouth, and I swallow him down.

He pants as he releases his grasp on my hair, his cock slipping out of my mouth. Cum and saliva slide down the corners of my mouth as I pant with need. Rev hums as his thumb collects some of the fluid, forcing it back into my mouth. I suck it off and he groans. "So beautiful."

Kas's hand rubs softly across the abused skin of my ass as he sets a slow pace. He begins to slowly thrust in and out of my ass, and I sob with my need for relief. Which has turned to actual physical pain at this point.

"You're going to come when I command, aren't you, Princess."

"Yes," I sob.

"Good." He slips a hand between us, his finger hovering over my clit. His movements are coordinated as he thrusts into my ass just as he pinches my clit. With one more smack to my ass, he commands, "Now!"

My scream echoes around the room as my body finally gets the release it has been begging for. My cunt clamps down on air as my thighs and the floor are soaked with my release. Kas echoes me, following with his own roar as he fills my ass with his seed. His heavy breathing matches my own while we try to catch our breaths.

He gently rubs a hand over my bare ass before pulling out with a grunt. He backs away for a moment only to spread my cheeks apart with a groan. "Your cum running down your legs, and my seed dripping out of your ass are enough to make my cock hard again."

I'm ripped away from Kas, then thrown over a shoulder. I look to find Bene stalking over to an altar. I'm about to ask what he's planning, but before I get the chance, I'm tossed on top of the altar. I hiss when the cold marble hits my bare back. Cum continues to leak out of me and onto the altar.

Bene stares down at me, which gives me time to take him in. He's completely bare, and his cock looks painfully hard as pre-cum seeps out, sliding down his shaft.

He groans, his voice strained when he says, "I don't know which hole to fuck."

I spread my legs, so he can take in my weeping holes. "I don't care which one you fuck, just pick one."

Black shadows explode around him as he pounces. He doesn't give me any warning before his cock spears my swollen cunt. I reach behind me to grip onto the edge of the altar as he begins to thrust without rhythm. There is nothing but frenzy and need with each snap of his hips as he bends to bite my lip.

"God, your pussy is strangling my dick, Dragoness." He groans as he runs his lips down my neck to feast on my breasts, and I wrap my legs around his waist, lifting my hips to meet his to force him deeper. My heels dig into his back, and he growls, fucking me harder.

He nips my nipple, and I moan, releasing my grip on the altar and moving to tangle my fingers in his hair. I pull his face deeper into my chest as I meet each of his thrusts. He releases my nipple with a pop, and he pants, "You love when your dragon loses control."

"Yes," I moan my agreement as he moves back to sucking and biting my nipples. He bites down on my breast as he thrusts in deep, hitting just the right spot to make stars bloom behind my eyes. He snarls as he slams into me, filling me with his cum.

I can feel our combined releases pool between my legs as he pulls out with a groan. I'm immediately flipped so that my belly is against the cool marble altar, and my legs hang over the edge with my ass and cunt on full display. My pussy is still fluttering as another cock slams into me. My fingers tighten around the edge of the altar as I hear Alair grunt. "So tight, Little Fox."

His cock feeds my pleasure, dragging out my orgasm when he pinches my clit, making my cunt tighten around his cock. With a groan, he pulls out of my tight channel. I'm about to whimper when I hear Dax laugh behind me.

I look up to find Alair now in front of me, and Dax has taken his place behind me. Alair's cock is soaked in my juices as he slips his thumb between my lips. He smirks as he says, "Open that needy mouth, Little Fox."

I do without hesitation, and he wastes no time slipping his wet cock between my lips. I can taste myself as well as the others, and I groan. Dax's cock teases my swollen pussy before he slams inside. I moan around Alair's cock, and his fingers tighten in my hair.

"Such a good queen." Dax grunts and starts to fuck me like a hungry animal. "Take my cock, Little Raven."

I moan as Alair starts to fuck my mouth, matching Dax's pace. Dax's fingers tighten on my hip, and he growls, "My fucking obsession."

"Yes," Alair pants. Fire builds in my abdomen as my pleasure starts to build again. Alair is the first to come as he jerks out of my mouth, coming over my chin and chest. His eyes look like liquid coal as tendrils of black swirl around us. His runs his fingers through the cum on my lips and presses it into my awaiting mouth. "You look downright devastating with my cum marking you."

I moan around his thumb as Dax lifts my hips to thrust in deeper. He snarls, his fingers digging harder into my hips, and I know I will have bruises there later. I bite Alair's thumb as fire explodes within me. Alair grunts as my cunt pulses around Dax. He sounds like a wild animal as he slams into me with a final roar. I feel impossibly full as I'm filled with even more cum. Eventually, my vision clears, and I look up from my position to find the others in front of me. Cum covers the floor as each of my men draw out the last of the pleasure.

I whimper as Dax pulls out. I'm still very sensitive due to the overwhelming orgasms drawn out of me. I collapse back onto the altar, too tired to move just yet.

Dax kisses a path up my spine before asking, "Are you well, Little Raven?"

A smile creases my face as I answer, "Never better."

I can hear the smile in his voice when he asks, "Is this the happy ending you wished for?"

I laugh. "Not even close. I never imagined I could feel the kind of happiness I do right now." I move just enough to look at Dax over my shoulder. "My happiness is immeasurable."

His smile is subtle, but he nods in satisfaction. "You don't regret falling for a bunch of villains?"

Groaning, I sit up to turn and wrap my arms around him. I hold him tight as I say, "I could never regret falling for any of you. Not when you have brought me so much love and happiness in return."

He hums as he wraps his arms around me. "Good. I wouldn't let you fly away anyway, Little Raven."

"You don't have to worry about me flying far, love." I pull away to find my other guys converging on Dax and me. To think this adventure started out so horribly and turned into something so wonderful. Love works in mysterious ways, but I never imagined it would be possible to capture the hearts and love of seven men.

A villain's love is obsessive and uncontrolled. Once you fall into their grasp, there is no return. I don't mind, though, because I know that my men love fiercely. They would rather watch the world burn to keep me than sacrifice me for the greater good. I wouldn't want it any other way.

So am I a villain or a hero? I'll let you decide.

We've been sucked into a book of fairytales, but something is different. This is darker... more sinister. The land is cursed, and all the villains are the rulers and are taking over everything, including the leading characters' hearts. The villain never gets the hearts of the leads but this time they will, and they will burn the world to the ground to keep them.

Join these authors as the villain takes it all.

Mania Balor – <u>His Destruction</u>

Stephanie Swann – <u>Poisonous Savage</u>

JS Mercier – <u>Sweet Addiction</u>

Mirabella Mooncrest – <u>His Pretty Prisoner</u>

Melanie True – <u>Beastly Beauty</u>

Ivy Cole – <u>The Stolen Throne</u>

Ella J. Black – <u>Double the Trouble</u>

About the Author

Ivy Cole is a longtime lover of writing and has wanted to publish her books for years. She loves Reverse Harem of many kinds. She's an indie author and can't wait to share future books with you.

Want to follow Ivy Cole and see future books? Follow her at:

https://www.facebook.com/groups/508646927449550/

Want all things, Ivy Cole? Click her Linktree to access all her social media accounts.

https://linktr.ee/ivycoleauthor

Also By

Books Also by Ivy Cole

Underground Syndicate Series:

Underworld

Tartarus

Why Choose Fables:

Meddling with Madness (Wonderland Retelling)

The Washington Wraiths

Ice Me Baby (Liz, Mac, Dean)